Keegan's Chronicles Book One

JULIA CRANE

Edited by Claire Teter
Cover art by Eden Crane Designs
Book formatting by CyberWitch Press

*For my husband
who never doubts and
always supports me.*

Chapter 1

Keegan unpacked her things, her mind on the photos of the weekend she had supposedly spent with Rourk. She wished she could remember him and the weekend at the cabin from before the trip to Ireland—a trip that had changed her life and erased her memories of him. The two of them looked so happy. So in love. As she picked up a pile of dirty clothes to toss into the laundry, a piece of paper fell out and drifted slowly to the floor.

She stared at it a moment, an inoffensive square of paper laying on the floor. Curious, she reached down and picked it up, her brow furrowed over her bright blue-green eyes. She opened it, smoothing the creases, and read:

Keegan, I am sorry I could not spend your special day with you. I will make it up to you. Forever Yours, Rourk

First the pictures and then the note— undeniable proof that she did, at one time, have a relationship with Rourk.

Keegan sighed, dropping the laundry to the floor without a thought as she flopped onto her back on the bed. Her pillow still smelled like her shampoo, despite the fact she had been gone for just over a week. The cool October breeze ruffled the sheer purple curtains at her window, making her shiver. She could smell the pine trees from the forest. It was so good to be home.

A thought struck her, and she leapt to her feet, rushing to her desk to grab her phone. It sat by her bendy desk lamp, between her camera and a couple of school books. She scrolled through the list of contacts and was annoyed to find Rourk's number was not on it. Strange. *Why wouldn't they have texted if they'd already met?*

Before she could talk herself out of it, she sent her father a text and asked for Rourk's number.

Rourk was miserable.

He hadn't bothered turning on the lights in his bedroom before he fell onto the bed, boots and all. Staring at the ceiling with his hands under his head, Rourk couldn't stop thinking about Keegan.

The battle in the fight for his kind was over, but it seemed yet another had just begun. He couldn't possibly accept the fact that his relationship with his chosen was over before it really began. There was no one else for him. Keegan was the only one.

He had to win her back.

Rourk ran his options through his head and realized there were only two. He could do nothing and hope Keegan's feelings for him would return, or he could take the human route and try to win her affections. He was not one to sit around and do nothing, so obviously it had to be option two.

His phone dinged on the nightstand and he reached over to grab it, flipping it open. It was a text from Keegan: *I'm sorry I don't remember you. I was looking at my photos and it looks like we had a gr8 weekend.*

Rourk sat up in bed and stared at the screen that held her message. His heart beat just a bit faster as he wracked his brain for the right words. The fact she had reached out to him first gave him hope.

Finally, he texted back: *It was the best weekend of my life. Would you like to go on a date this weekend?*

Her response was almost instantaneous. *A date? What did you have in mind?*

Rourk dropped his phone to the bed and groaned, shoving both hands through his hair as he stood. Glancing around his room, he hoped for sudden inspiration. He paced a couple steps, hating how awkward he felt, and tried to think of something to say that didn't sound lame. It had been much easier when the bond was there and no thought was required. But he knew anything worthwhile took effort, and Keegan was worth it.

He paced back and forth three times in his small bedroom before he finally picked up his phone and tapped out his response: *I know it's not original, but how does dinner and a movie sound?*

Almost as soon as it left his screen, she answered: *GR8 :)*

I'll pick you up Friday at 6. Goodnight.

Night.

Texting would take some getting used to. Rourk wondered how she texted so much and so fast. Before the great battle, when he had watched Keegan to keep her safe, she was always attached to her phone. In his opinion, picking up the phone and having an actual conversation would be easier. *The things you do for love*, he thought with a grin.

He could do this. After all, Rourk thought with a wry grin, he was a battle-hardened warrior.

Back in her room, Keegan laid her phone back down with a smile.

This could be fun; after all, he was cute.

Chapter 2

It was strange for her to go back to school after so much had happened. She had battled and she had *died*! *How does a girl go back to normal after that?*

Walking through the front doors of the school felt surreal. Her classmates mingled at their lockers, chatting and laughing like average students. Keegan felt so disconnected. She was positive they'd never taken part in a battle or watched men and women die in the fight for their race.

They had never killed others to save themselves.

Keegan's brother, Thaddeus, had filled her in on the outcome of the battle, so she was aware now that many of her friends were also creatures of the light. They weren't elves, but they weren't human either. She wasn't sure if she felt relieved by that fact or upset. She had liked thinking she was the only special one among all the humans.

Keegan walked down the fluorescent-lit hall and felt as if everyone was staring at her, but she convinced herself it was all in her head. She was self-conscious, absently smoothing her auburn hair and tugging at the hem of her school skirt. When she got to her locker, she was happy to see things looked as they always did and for the first time since she arrived at school, she felt like herself.

Lauren, Anna, and Katie were gathered by her locker, books in hand while they gossiped, and the boys were messing around as usual. Keegan couldn't help but steal a glance at Donald as she walked by, and she noticed his eyes were on her as well. They both laughed and looked away, Keegan's face flushing. Was it just her imagination or had he gotten even hotter since she saw him last? He was tall and lean with a runner's build, and his orange hair was just so cute standing up all over the place, the craziness punctuated by the fact that his white Oxford shirt wasn't buttoned right. His eyes were a crazy blue. What was she thinking?

Forget about Donald, he's not even interested in you.

Keegan had managed to run late for school. No sooner than she had opened her mouth to greet her friends, the bell rang to signal the start of classes. She frowned.

"We'll talk later," Anna told her. Keegan's best friend was rocking her individuality with a purple and lime green striped scarf over her school sweater and white tights. Her pretty, oval face was perfectly made up with shimmery lavender eye shadow and pale pink lip gloss; her cat-like eyes were lined with silver.

Keegan leaned to give her a quick hug before she ran off to class.

"It's good to see you," Lauren said and squeezed Keegan's arm affectionately. Keegan noticed her friend had gotten her dark, curly hair cut; not much, but just noticeable. Lauren was in her cheerleading uniform, her long legs still tanned from the summer. "We'll meet you at lunch."

"Bye, Keegan." Katie gave her a shy wave and followed after Lauren.

Homeroom passed in a blur. Mrs. Harris had to repeat Keegan's name three times during attendance at the beginning of class. The student seated next to her, a slight girl with mocha-colored skin and huge, dark eyes, had to elbow Keegan to wake her from her thoughts.

Donald cornered her in the hall before first period so they could talk in private. "I never got a chance to thank you for saving my life," he said. He looked down as if he were embarrassed, the toe of one of his Chucks scuffing the floor.

"It was my mother that really saved you," Keegan shrugged. "I was just the foolish one to rush into the middle of a battlefield."

His incredible blue eyes moved to hers. "So you really died, huh? What was that like? Did you see the other side? Do you feel different now that you're back in our world?"

Keegan knew those were the questions everyone wanted to ask her, but didn't dare.

"I don't recall it at all," Keegan told him apologetically. "I know that's not the exciting answer everyone would like to hear. But if I hadn't been told I died, I would have never known. I do feel a little different. My body temperature seems lower now, and I'm always cold. And apparently my bond to my chosen has been broken. Other than that, I feel like the same old Keegan."

Donald stepped back, his eyes widening. *Did he just hear correctly? The bond was broken?* Suddenly, he felt very nervous and unsure of himself. His palms were sweating. He didn't even trust himself to speak.

"Are you okay?" Keegan asked with a frown. "You don't look so well."

"Sorry, I need to go. I'm glad you're alive, and thanks again for saving my life." He stumbled away.

Donald shoved his hands in his pockets, his eyes on the dirty linoleum floor as he hurried down the hall. He had dreamed of this moment; a chance with Keegan. Yet, when it was staring him in the face, he ran away like a scared, lovesick loser. *Real smooth, Donald.*

Chemistry class passed slowly. Usually, it was Keegan's favorite class, but she just felt antsy. There was too much on her mind. She sat and watched the second hand go around and around, wondering what in the world had gotten into Donald.

She really needed to catch up with Anna and Lauren because it seemed like forever since they had talked. They always sat together at lunch; she was eager to reach them. After suffering through a boring history lecture, it was finally lunch time.

She practically ran for her locker to get rid of

her books, and slammed into Spencer and Sam in the hallway.

"Whoa, slow down Keegan. I feel like I've been hit by a bulldozer." Spencer rubbed his shoulder. He was a skinny guy whose long limbs made him seem tall, and a head full of black hair. He crossed his bright green eyes.

Sam, a good-looking blonde, laughed.

"Hey guys, I can't talk right now! I'm in a hurry," she told them quickly, waving as she dashed off once more.

They stared at her as she sprinted down the hallway to her locker. Other students parted to make way for her. Spencer and Sam glanced at each other and shook their heads.

Once at her locker, Keegan impatiently waited for Anna and Lauren. She drummed her fingers on the beige metal and looked at her watch. *Where were they?*

Anna got there first. She gave Keegan a cheesy grin as she walked up.

"Oh thank God, I didn't think you were ever going to show up," Keegan said with a sigh, leaning against her locker wearily.

Looking at Keegan like she was crazy, Anna responded, "I got here as soon as I could. The bell just rang. Chill out."

Lauren sauntered down the hall a second later. Anna and Keegan laughed as they watched all the guys turn and stare at her legs as she walked by. Lauren shook her hips deliberately— she loved the attention.

"Hey. Ready for lunch?" she asked with a grin.

"Let's go outside to eat so we can catch up in

private," Keegan said. She grabbed them by the arms and pulled them towards the door.

Keegan noticed a glance exchanged between Anna and Lauren, and wondered what that was all about. Shrugging it off, she led the way through the back doors of the school.

It was a brilliantly bright day with not a cloud in sight. Some of their classmates lounged around the quad with their lunches and sodas, enjoying the mild weather and sunshine. Laughter and the distant thrum of cars on the main road were the only sounds as the girls headed for the shade of an old oak tree.

Once they were hidden behind the bushes surrounding the tree, Keegan turned with her hands planted on her hips. "So. How long have you guys known I wasn't human?"

Lauren looked down sheepishly, unable to make eye contact. Anna's smile was ear to ear. "Finally! Do you know how hard it's been *all these years* to not be able to talk about the elephant in the room?"

Keegan wasn't sure if she should laugh or cry, or stomp her feet like a little kid while screaming not fair! She settled for crossing her arms over her chest and narrowing her eyes at her friends. "You've both known all this time?"

Anna shrugged her shoulders. "Hey, it's not our fault that elves like to be so secretive."

"So, you're a fairy?" Keegan turned her attention to Lauren.

Lauren looked from side to side to make sure no one was looking. Suddenly, star-like flecks appeared in the air and translucent wings flapped open behind her. Flapping her wings, Lauren floated into the air with a big grin across her face.

"Wow, that is really neat!" Keegan turned to Anna. "What's your story? I hear people aren't quite sure about you because your dad is human?"

Anna lifted her hands in the air and closed her eyes. Keegan's mouth dropped open as flames appeared in her palms.

Keegan jumped up and down, clapping, and squealed, "We are like the coolest kids ever!"

Anna's face scrunched up. "I don't know. I think Calvron might be the coolest kid ever."

Lauren nodded her head in agreement. "He is awesome!"

Keegan crossed her arms tightly across her chest and stared back and forth at them. It wasn't fair that they all knew about each other and she was the only one left out. They were supposed to be her friends! She gave in and asked, "Why is he so cool?"

Smiling mysteriously, Lauren said, "He's a very powerful wizard, and they're rare these days. He can do almost anything; at least, that's how it seems."

Anna looked wistful. "I wish I had a quarter of his power."

"What exactly are you, Anna?" Keegan raised an eyebrow. "You're not a spirit walker like your mom, are you?"

Anna's eyes narrowed. "How did you know my mom is a spirit walker?"

Keegan was momentarily stunned into silence. "You guys didn't hear?"

They exchanged another glance, this time a confused one. Anna shook her head. "Hear what?"

Taking a deep breath, Keegan told them the long version of how she lost and regained her life. They both stared at her with their mouths hanging open.

"You guys know about the battle between the light and dark elves, right?"

Anna's face fell and she nodded. "Yeah, we heard something about it."

"Well, I was there," Keegan said. She gave them a wry grin as they both gasped.

Lauren covered her mouth with one hand and touched Keegan's shoulder with the other.

"So were Donald and the other guys. Donald was hurt, and I ran onto the field to help him. My mom is a Healer, and she was able to treat his wounds, but we were in the middle of the fighting." Keegan paused, clearing her throat as she remembered the clash of old-fashioned weaponry, the stench of hundreds of sweating bodies, and the ground drenched in blood. "I was hit by an arrow and killed."

Anna and Lauren looked at her in horror, but Keegan plunged on. "Anna, your mom somehow knew I was dead and showed up. She brought me back to life with dark magic."

When Keegan finished, Lauren spoke first. "Oh my god, you were dead? Keegan, you were dead!" She pulled Keegan into a tight hug. "I can't believe we could have lost you for good."

Anna was quiet for several moments before she whispered, "My mom knows dark magic?"

Neither Lauren nor Keegan knew what to say. The look on Anna's face made Keegan swiftly change the subject. "What do you guys know about elves?" She was curious if they really knew anything, and if so, whether any of it was accurate. She also wanted to clear the gloom that had followed her story.

Lauren bounced up and down. "I've heard that elves put on a front that they live among humans, but in reality they live underground. Is that true?"

Keegan couldn't help but smile. "There is a sliver of truth. We have underground safe houses in case of emergencies. Elves prefer living in nature over living in a city."

Anna finally spoke up, her voice a little clearer than it had been moments before. "Well, we're all envious that elves have the key to finding your perfect partner. We think that is the real reason you're all so secretive. Although, we really wish elves would share what they know. It doesn't seem fair they're the only ones that know their soul mates without the search."

Anna's observation brought all of Keegan's problems back to the surface, and she pouted.

What's wrong?" Anna demanded, reaching to shake Keegan's shoulder gently.

"It's true about the perfect partner. We call them our 'chosen' since they are chosen for us at birth. We aren't supposed to meet them until we turn eighteen. Apparently, I have already met my chosen, but because of the dark magic I don't recall him." It felt good to finally have someone to talk to about it all; it was so confusing for her. She pulled out her phone and showed them a picture she had saved on it of her and Rourk near the waterfall. She explained how they had spent the weekend together and she couldn't remember.

"When I was brought back," Keegan said,

shooting a glance at Anna. "I met him, and I felt nothing for him." Keegan could tell by the looks on her friends' faces that they felt badly for her. People searched high and low for their perfect match. To have it handed to you and then taken away seemed too cruel.

"He's hot." Anna grinned and handed the phone back to Keegan, who managed a weak smile. Dropping her eyes, Anna continued. "You asked what I was, because of my parents. Well, I'm a witch." She fidgeted with her sweater. After a brief pause, she added, "On the side of the light."

Keegan could tell Anna was bothered about her mother knowing dark magic.

"I wonder if there are any spells to bring back the bond?" Anna said. "It would seem if it was taken away that it could be given back."

For the first time, Keegan allowed herself to feel hopeful. "Do you really think that is possible?"

"I will have to look into it. There is still so much I don't know, and I've never had anyone to teach me. Maybe I can talk to Calvron; he might be able to help or at least point me in the right direction."

Keegan glanced down at the photo one more time before she put her phone away. "Thank you, Anna; you have no idea how much this means to me."

Keegan was excited and relieved that she could finally share who she *really* was with her best friends. She wondered if this was why they had stayed friends no matter how different their personalities were. Perhaps creatures of the light could sense one another. Keegan smiled and thought of all the times she had made up stories in her mind of people and guessed whether they were creatures or human. Not once had she given thought to the fact that her friends might not be. Oh, the irony of it.

A huge smile spread across her face. She couldn't wait to see what adventures they would share together now that their powers were out in the open.

Chapter 3

Rourk looked through his closet trying to decide what to wear. It was their first date and he wanted it to be perfect, but he had no idea what humans usually wore for such things.

He pushed his hangers further to the left. Then again to the right; his wardrobe was useless. There had to be something for him to wear. All of his clothes looked alike: the shirts were all earth tones and he had a few pairs of jeans and khakis. He smiled and thought, *Keegan would probably love to take me shopping.*

His father came to the door and stared in at Rourk. The gray hair at his Greg's temples had gotten lighter since the battle, though it only heightened his movie-star good looks. Every time he looked at his dad, Rourk marveled at how different they were.

His father pointedly stared at the clothes strewn across the bed. "What are you doing?"

Embarrassed, Rourk answered, "Trying to

figure out what to wear."

His father's booming laugh filled the room, shocking him. The man barely ever smiled, let alone laughed. "Son, in eighteen years I have never seen you debate on clothing choices."

Rourk's shoulders slumped. He took a deep breath and closed his eyes. "Dad, this sucks. How do humans deal with this on a regular basis? I'm nervous, what's up with that? I'm a warrior, we do not get nervous, let alone over a silly date."

Greg placed a hand on Rourk's shoulder, catching his son's gray eyes with his own intense blues. "I'm sorry this isn't going as easy as you expected. Just know that it will be worth it in the long run."

His dad walked away with a knowing grin on his face, which rather annoyed Rourk.

Finally, Rourk decided to play it safe and picked a pair of khaki pants and a plain black t-shirt. Looking in the mirror, he ran his hand through his rust colored hair; he needed a haircut. He rubbed his face vigorously and thought, *Well, there isn't much I can do about my looks.* Keegan had found him attractive before the black magic, so hopefully that hadn't changed.

Grabbing his keys from his dresser, he headed out. As he drove towards her house, his stomach was in knots. *What's wrong with me? It's just a date.*

The doorbell rang, and Keegan's father yelled out his usual line: "Don't forget the first rule of dating."

"Dad, you say that every time I go on a date. You know it gets old." Laughing, she added, "If he breaks that rule, it's your fault since you trained him."

Keegan glanced at herself once more in the mirror and thought, *Not bad*. Her auburn hair was behaving itself. She had on just the right amount of makeup to bring out her features. She had chosen to wear a form-fitting blue sweater and a pair of jeans that flattered her figure.

She opened the door, hoping to feel a spark or something. Yet again, she felt nothing.

He was hot, she would give him that. They made eye contact. His grey eyes were so intense, and she loved how strong his jaw line was. She gave him a once over, thinking to herself, *Nice*. She always thought guys looked hot in khakis. His shirt was just tight enough to show off his defined chest. The sleeves looked a little snug; she tried not to stare at his muscled arms.

"Keegan, you look...um, you look good." He stared at the porch at his feet as if he were embarrassed. The sky was rose-colored behind him, a beautiful contrast to the trees surrounding the house. Keegan loved the way it smelled outside when fall had arrived.

She smiled at him. "Thank you." *You look good? That was the best he had? Ugh, this might be a long night after all.*

"So, where are we going to eat?" she asked, twirling a piece of her hair. She hadn't stepped back to let him in the house, nor had she moved forward to the porch. Of course, she didn't notice his confusion over it.

"I figured we'd keep it low key and grab a pizza. If that's ok with you?"

"That sounds great!" Her smile reached her

eyes causing them to sparkle.

Rourk didn't think he would ever get used to her overwhelming beauty. She was perfection. Why couldn't he say the words? *Good?* That didn't begin to do her justice. He was going to have to do better than that if he was going to win her back. Why did he feel so awkward? It was not supposed to be this way. When they had been together before it felt so natural, as if they had known each other their entire lives. He would do anything to get that back.

They rode to the restaurant in silence, and not the pleasant kind. Rourk tried to think of something interesting to talk about. Finally, he thought of a topic he knew interested her. "How is your photography going? Have you gotten any good shots lately?"

He was relieved to see her face light up. When she excitedly started rambling on about how much she loved taking pictures, Rourk knew he'd found the right conversation starter.

"I really want to get a new lens so I can get better pictures of animals in their natural environment," Keegan said, her words coming fast. "My parents have been talking about going to Sri Lanka, and I'd love to get some good shots of the elephants. If I'm lucky, maybe a tiger."

Rourk tensed at the mention of a tiger, even though he knew it was a well known fact there were tigers in Sri Lanka.

"When are you planning on going to Sri Lanka?"

"I'm not sure. My parents tend to spring trips on us out of nowhere. Hopefully soon."

"How many countries have you been to?" It was hard to keep his eyes on the road when he wanted so badly to watch her face as she spoke.

Keegan paused to think and counted off on her fingers silently. "At least fourteen, but I've probably missed some. I only count the ones I can remember and not the ones from when I was a baby. What about you? Do you like to travel?"

Rourk shook his head. "I haven't been many places. My father doesn't enjoy traveling anymore. Not since my mother died." He didn't want to travel down that path. Glancing at Keegan, he went on. "Do you have a favorite place you have been?"

Keegan tapped a finger to her lips. "Hmm, I think that would have to be Nepal. It's so beautiful there, and the people are so friendly even though they live in poverty. It's cool to see how the women dress in bright colors and always have smiles on their faces. The hiking is amazing there too. I think you would love it."

Her thoughtfulness touched him. "I'm sure I would. I love hiking. I think that's pretty common among elves."

"That's true." She settled back in the seat. "Although, after the first time I went to Nepal, I couldn't eat chicken for a long time. They slaughter them right in the open, like on the sidewalks. Probably one of the reasons I went on that vegetarian kick you mentioned."

He could listen to her talk for hours.

Rourk pulled his truck into the parking lot of the pizza shop and put it into park. He hurriedly walked around to let Keegan out, but she had already hopped from the cab and was waiting for him next to her door.

Michael's Pizza was one of Keegan's favorites, though she didn't think Rourk knew that. It was packed with people she recognized from school. The servers bounced from table to table amid the chaos, white smiles plastered across every face. Keegan took a deep breath and felt her stomach rumble.

Once they were seated, Rourk asked, "What kind of pizza do you want?"

"Meat lover's. I'm starving."

Rourk wasn't sure why this bothered him so much. He had found it somewhat annoying when he had first learned she was a vegetarian. To have her forget about that reminded him how she had forgotten about him, as well. If only he could turn the clock back to their time in the cabin, when he had gladly cooked her vegetarian meals, and she had looked at him as if he was the only person on the planet. Now, she was glancing around the room as if she was bored.

Rourk watched as Keegan devoured four pieces of pizza. "You weren't kidding when you said you were hungry."

"It's just sooo good." Keegan wiped her face with the napkin. "I love pizza. Actually, I love most food."

Looking up from his own slice, he smiled.

"You have earned my father's approval for a second date, by the way."

Somewhat surprised, he said, "Well, I would hope so." He was her chosen after all, and he had fought alongside her father in the Great Battle.

Keegan let him in on the inside joke. "He tells me that if I'm on a date and the guy sits with his back to the door, I'm supposed to get up and leave."

Rourk laughed. He could clearly picture Richard making up this rule. He was a character—and a great man. "Well, you don't have to worry. I will always make your safety my number one priority."

Keegan liked the sound of that. She really needed to give him a chance. Just then, while the two of them were having what felt like a great moment, her phone buzzed in her purse. She was surprised when she saw the text was from Donald, and her heart skipped a beat. He rarely texted her.

The text said, *A bunch of us are going to play laser tag. Do you want to come?*

Grinning, she replied, *Wish I could but on a date.*

Date? Who's the lucky guy?

Feeling herself blush, she replied, *My chosen.*

How's that going?

Keegan looked across the table at Rourk who was eyeing his piece of pizza. She replied, *Strange*

Have fun, maybe next time you can join us.

Love to, she replied, sad to stop the conversation.

Rourk took a sip of his drink. "Was that Anna or Lauren?"

After a brief pause, "Yeah, it was Anna. She was just seeing what was up." *Why did I just lie to him? You're never supposed to lie to your chosen.* Keegan felt like crying. Why was this not going as it was supposed to? Was she ever going to have feelings for this stranger sitting across from her?

They went to the movies after eating. She had

to admit the movie was funny, and it was nice to know Rourk had a sense of humor. She eventually managed to relax and enjoy herself.

After the night was over, Rourk pulled down the long drive to her house and parked out front, cutting the engine. He jumped from the car and hurried to her side. Taking her hand, he walked her to the door.

Keegan wondered if he was going to try to kiss her. She didn't have to wonder long.

Stopping before they even reached the doorway, he put his hand under her hair, and pulled her towards him. He kissed her softly at first, and then with more force. Abruptly he pulled away. As he stared down at her, he almost looked frightened. "Did you feel it?"

Startled, she asked, "Feel what?"

Rourk groaned inwardly. A part of him had hoped that kissing her would make her feel the electricity they had felt before. His mind was reeling.

The bond was actually gone for her. He recalled their first kiss and her reaction. *"Wow, did you feel that?" she had asked.* Now, she felt nothing.

Of course, for him it was still the same as before.

Keegan patted him awkwardly on the arm. "Ok, well, I had fun. Maybe we can go out again sometime?"

"I hope so," he murmured, bereft as she pulled away from him.

Rourk watched as she walked into her house—she didn't even look back.

Keegan went straight to her room through the darkened house; everyone was already in bed and she didn't want to wake them.

She thought about the evening as she got undressed. He truly wasn't *that* bad. But, could she see herself spending the rest of her life with him? That—she wasn't sure of. She figured time would tell. There was no precedence for their situation as far as she knew. Would she still be expected to marry him when she turned eighteen, even if there was no bond? She couldn't picture her mother making her marry someone against her will. She pulled on her favorite polar bear pajamas and threw her hair in a pony tail.

She pulled out her phone and stared at the screen; she still couldn't believe Donald had texted her. After a slight internal debate, she sent him a text.

How was laser tag?

Fun, we dominated.

Of course, you are magical creatures.

Not as magical as you.

Keegan had to physically stop herself from squealing, bouncing on the tips of her toes in the dark and clutching the phone to her chest. *OMG*, he said she was magical, and at the pizza place, he had asked who the lucky guy was. Could he possibly be interested in her?

Okay, calm down; she knew Donald liked to joke around. Maybe he was just being funny.

I wish I had been there, Keegan wrote.

Me too, see you on Monday at school.

Keegan finished getting ready for bed and finally got under the covers, turning over on her back to stare at the ceiling in thought. So much had changed in such a short period of time. She felt as if her whole world had been turned upside down.

Why did things have to get so complicated? This was supposed to be easy! She was supposed to turn eighteen and marry her chosen— something she had been planning on since she found out his name was Rourk. She had lain awake many nights dreaming about their perfect home. They were going to have a dog—a fat, lazy English bulldog and his name was going to be Santa. She liked to humor herself and thought it would be funny since humans think Santa and elves go hand in hand. She figured they would have at least three kids. It was going to be perfect.

Why did this have to happen?

Now, without the bond, the thought of getting married at eighteen seemed absurd. That was only a year away. She had college to think about. She'd dreamed of going to college in Alaska, because they had one of the best marine biology programs and her dream was to work with dolphins. It had never crossed her mind whether Rourk would even want to move to Alaska.

Closing her eyes, Keegan let sleep take over; she would worry about it all later.

Chapter 4

Anna was nervous, but she needed answers. She had already put it off too long.

Thankfully, her mother seemed to have come out of her depression fog. It felt like it hadn't been all that long since her mom had been nearly frozen with despair, unable to function or even smile. She had done a complete turnabout.

Actually, Anna could not recall a time when her mom had seemed as happy. Maybe she was on a new medication or something. Whatever it was, Anna was glad for it. Her mom was back to doing her hair and make-up, and she had even been going for morning runs like she used to before things got bad.

The idea of upsetting her mother made Anna's stomach roll, but it couldn't be avoided. She took the stairs slowly, dreading the confrontation and what it could bring.

Her mom stood in the kitchen arranging an assortment of red and yellow flowers in her favorite blue glass vase. A private smile crossed her face as Anna watched, and she wondered what her mother was thinking. "Hey, Mom."

Jennifer glanced up at her daughter, standing in the doorway. Anna was more subdued than usual, wearing only a pair of blue jeans and a tank top. Her pink hair was secured with a bland gray headband.

"What's wrong?" she asked, not bothering with pleasantries.

"We need to talk," Anna said softly.

Her mother's smile disappeared as she turned to face Anna fully, her hands moving away from the flowers. "I take it you've talked to Keegan?"

Anna was surprised. She thought she was going to have to pull it out of her mother one word at a time. "Yes, and she told me you know black magic? Mom, how can that be? I don't understand any of this."

Sighing, Jennifer walked forward and grabbed her daughter's hands, squeezing them tightly. Her dark eyes were haunted. "Let's sit down."

Anna let her mother lead her to the table. She watched as Jennifer bustled to the refrigerator and pulled out a glass pitcher of juice.

Anna tried to remember the last time she'd seen her mom look so youthful. Even just wearing a pair of gray cotton yoga pants and an old, worn out T-shirt on her tall, willowy body, Anna's mom was beautiful. She had her long brown hair pulled into a high ponytail that swished around her neck when she moved. Her toenails were painted pink.

Jennifer put a glass in front of Anna and sat

across from her. "Anna, you know I was raised by your great-grandmother and that she was also a witch." She cleared her throat, shifting uncomfortably in her seat. "What I failed to mention was that she was a dark witch."

Anna stared at her mother in disbelief, her hands wrapped around her glass even though she hadn't picked it up yet. "My great-grandmother was a dark witch? How is that even possible?"

"It's a long story, or at least the story unfolded over a long period of time." She paused, and then held up a finger. "One minute."

Raising an eyebrow at her mother, Anna watched as she hurried from the room, her flip-flops making slapping sounds on the linoleum. She returned a minute later with a large leather-bound album and opened it on the tabletop. She flipped forward a few pages until she came to a picture of a handsome young man in old-timey clothes. "Your great-grandfather, as you know, was also a spirit walker."

"That's him?" Anna murmured, leaning forward to stare at his face. He had a mischievous glint in his dark eyes and hair the exact shade of Jennifer's.

Jennifer nodded. "Yes. His name was Patrick. As a spirit walker, his body absorbed the spirits he took over to the other side. He was unable to protect himself from it because he was never taught to shield himself, or at least that's what we liked to believe." Her mother's eyes darkened. "Some wondered if he let his guard down on purpose because he enjoyed the power of absorbing souls. One man with thousands of souls. You can imagine all the demons that came along with that. It was feared he was going mad. He started acting irrational. His mind shattered, and he became a deranged lunatic that could no longer live among the humans. It was as if the souls were speaking through him, comparable to someone with split personalities. Of course, your great-grandmother, Grace, loved him very much and it killed her to see him fall apart. She tried every spell she could think of and nothing worked. She searched near and far trying to find a cure." Jennifer flipped a few pages in the photo album to show Anna a picture of a vibrantly beautiful young woman in a long black dress. She looked just like Jennifer.

Her mother stopped and looked out the small kitchen window, her eyes distant, before she continued. "She heard about a dark witch that could help her. Light and dark witches do not communicate with each other. So, Grace cast a spell on herself to appear as if she were a young dark witch. She begged the dark witch to teach her the ways of the dark. The witch was so impressed with your great-grandmother's skills at such a young age that she took her under her wing."

She leaned over and grabbed Anna's hand. "I know this is a lot to take in."

"Just finish the story, Mom." Anna pulled her hand away.

"She was gone for years, and when she returned, Patrick was dead. She went berserk and cursed the light. She swore never to return, and she remained a dark witch until her death. Unfortunately, she passed on her skills to me. I was not told of her story until after she passed away. A kind, light witch took care of me until I was of age. She taught me the beauty of the light."

Anna sat with her mouth open, staring dumbfounded at her mom. "You should have told me. How could you have kept this from me all these years?"

"What good would that have done? I am not a witch. I am a spirit walker."

Anna glared at her. "All these years, you have left me on my own to deal with my power. You have given me no guidance." She pushed back from the table and crossed her arms.

Her mother's anger filled the room, though she tried to hold it in. "What did you expect me to do? Teach my daughter black magic?"

"Well, no, but it would have been nice to have known about all of this." Anna shifted uncomfortably. "Mom, I need to learn about my powers. I'm almost eighteen and this is crazy. I don't know what you're trying to shield me from. Avoiding it isn't going to make me human."

Jennifer's face was pained. She looked away quickly, but not before Anna saw the tears gathered in her mother's eyes. "I'm sorry, Anna, I know I haven't been fair to you and my reasons have been purely selfish. I was really hoping you were going to be a normal human. I thought maybe since your father was human…"

"We've known for years that I'm not *normal*, as you say." There was a lot more bitterness in her words than she meant.

"We'll sort this out, Anna. I'm sorry, and you are right. You need someone to guide you in your abilities."

There was an awkward pause while the two

of them stared across the open album at each other.

"Mother, the real reason I wanted to talk to you is because of Keegan," Anna started slowly, her hands clasped on the table. She stared down at her chipped blue nail polish. "When you brought her back, you took away her bond to her chosen."

"I know, and there is nothing I can do about that."

Looking at her mom searchingly, Anna said, "Are you sure? If you can take something away, there must be a way to give it back?"

"Anna, I'm sorry. Dark magic is not known for its kindness. Losing her bond is a small price to pay for her life. She will be fine." Jennifer took a sip of her juice, entirely too calm and collected for Anna.

"Sure, just like *you're* fine? Look how great your marriage is working out for you. Elves are the only ones that have this secret to finding their perfect match. Do you really think it's fair to take away Keegan's chance at happiness?"

Her mom stared intently at her fingers, avoiding her daughter's gaze. "Anna, I truly am unable to help her. I wish I could." She looked up, her soft brown eyes catching her daughter's. "However, there might be someone that can. The light witch that took me in has since passed to the other side. She does have a daughter, Magdalena, who happens to be an extremely powerful witch. She might know of a spell that could reverse the damage I caused to the bond."

Anna breathed a little easier, closing her eyes as she allowed herself a bit of hope that she could help her best friend. Not only might she be able to help Keegan but she was finally going to meet a light witch. Perhaps the woman would give her the guidance she had ached for.

"Where does she live?"

Jennifer frowned. "Well, that's the tricky part—I am not sure. It might take me a while to track her down. I will start making inquiries right away. Anna, don't get your hopes up. It is very likely that it's not reversible. Please don't tell Keegan and give her false hope. She needs to start accepting the fact that it may never return. It would be cruel to make her think otherwise until you have concrete information."

"I won't say anything to Keegan." Anna looked over at her mom. "I'm really glad this is all out in the open now. I have so many questions, I don't even know where to begin. I have to say it's kinda cool that my mom knows black magic."

"As much as I've wanted you to think I'm cool over the years, this is not the way I wanted it to happen," her mother answered wryly, raising an eyebrow at her daughter pointedly. "Black magic can be very dangerous, Anna."

"I know, Mom. I don't want to learn black magic. I want to learn the ways of the light witch. I want you to be proud of me." Anna was kind of embarrassed to admit it.

"Honey, I have always been proud of you."

Anna smiled, relieved. She went on, "You seem to be happier lately. Are you and Dad doing better? I haven't heard you fight in awhile."

"No, actually, we aren't. I just feel better about myself and have realized I don't need to be married to be happy. Keegan's mother gave me a healing, and I feel like my old self again. It's such a wonderful feeling." Jennifer reached across the table to touch Anna's hand. "Honey, there is something you need to know."

"What?"

"Your father and I will be filing for divorce soon."

Anna took her hand away from her mom's and crossed her arms across her chest, her heart pounding. "That sucks, Mom."

"I'm sorry, Anna. I *have* tried."

"I know you have," Anna sighed, resting her elbows on the table and putting her face in her hands. "I've been expecting you guys to divorce for years. I wish Dad wasn't such a jerk to you."

"It's not really his fault. It isn't easy for humans to be involved with the gifted."

"That's a lame excuse. Why are you still sticking up for him?" Anna looked up with a glare, letting her palms rest on the tabletop.

"He's your father, and I will always love him," Jennifer said simply, shrugging. "Speaking of humans, any progress with Xavier?"

"Nice job on the subject switch. There hasn't been any progress. He just doesn't see me as anything more than a friend. I think he's interested in a cheerleader at school." Anna's lower lip jutted out in a pout.

"I'm sorry, honey. I know you care about him. Maybe you should start dating someone."

"Sure, the guys are knocking down my door." Anna rolled her eyes at her mom.

"Why wouldn't they be? You are beautiful, intelligent and original."

"It's the last one, Mom. Not all guys are into

chicks that change their hair color at the drop of the hat and don't conform to society." Anna pushed her recently dyed pink fringe behind her ear.

"Well, it's their loss." Jennifer gave her a beautiful grin.

"Of course, you aren't biased or anything," Anna joked, taking a sip of her juice. It was some kind of grape juice, and it had gotten warm while they talked.

"Of course not. Do you want something to eat?" Her mom stood and moved to the fridge, opening the door and bending to shuffle through its contents.

"Sure, what are you making?"

"How about a grilled cheese sandwich?"

"Ah, yeah! How could I turn that down?"

Jennifer was silent as she pulled out the cheese, bread, and butter. As she put the skillet on the burner and turned it on, she said, "Anna, I'm glad we had this talk. I really hope Magdelena can help you get the bond back. Keegan does deserve to be happy. Although, I really think she can find happiness without the bond."

"It's worth looking into," Anna replied. "I feel kinda responsible since my mother is the one that broke the bond."

"Don't forget I also saved her life."

Anna watched her mom butter two slices of bread and slice the cheese, before tossing the sandwich in the skillet. She told her mother, "I can't imagine life without Keegan. It still doesn't seem real that she died. It's just so bizarre. Thank you for brining her back."

"I'm glad I was able to help. Keegan is a good

girl."

When her grilled cheese was done, Jennifer placed it in front of her and they chatted about school while Anna finished off the sandwich.

On the table at her elbow, her phone buzzed loudly. It was a text from Calvron. *Time to play.*

"Thanks for the food and the talk, Mom. I'm so excited to meet Magdalena. I'm going to go hang out with the guys."

Jennifer waved her off. "All right, well have fun, and I will let you know as soon as I hear anything. We'll talk more about this later."

Grabbing her phone as she ran up to her room to change, Anna replied, *Can Keegan come?*

Of course

K, see you soon

She sent a quick text to Keegan, *On my way over, we're going on an adventure.*

Chapter 5

An adventure? Keegan loved surprises.

She got up from the couch where she had been idly flipping through television channels and ran upstairs to change.

Adventures usually required sneakers. Keegan grabbed her Puma trail shoes and threw on a pair of jeans along with a band tee. She grabbed a hoodie since she was always cold. She didn't bother with make-up.

Running down the stairs, she yelled to her parents, "Going out with Anna!"

As she opened the door, Anna's old, rusty Buick pulled into the driveway. Keegan yanked open the door and said, "Good timing!" Jumping in the car, she excitedly asked "So, where are we going?"

"Right now, we're going to get Lauren, and after that you will officially be invited into the club." Anna had her pink hair tucked under a lacy white beret and was wearing an electric red cardigan sweater with black skinny jeans that had glittery hearts on one leg. She signaled as she turned out of the long, gravel driveway that led back to Keegan's house and took a left onto the main road.

Keegan glanced over at her profile. "What club?"

"We call it the ABC club," Anna flashed a grin. "Amazingly Beautiful Creatures."

They had a club and she wasn't aware of it? *How could they keep all these secrets from her?* Keegan's anger began to build; she had noticed she got angry more often lately. When she started to get mad, her body felt colder. She normally tried to think happy thoughts right away, which warmed her back up. Reminding herself that at least she was invited now, she was very curious to see what it was all about. Instead of responding, she just turned to stare out the window at the passing scenery.

Lauren was waiting in her own driveway, looking like a star as usual. Her Hollister sweater was pale peach and form fitting and her khaki corduroys were perfectly pressed over her leather slip-on shoes. She slid into the backseat with a bright greeting.

They headed out of town down a winding, two-lane road beneath a bright and clear autumn sky. In the distance, Keegan watched the Appalachians draw nearer, a never-ending sea of fiery, rolling hills. Every so often, her family would pack a lunch and drive to the mountains to go hiking for the day. The Appalachians always felt so magical and surreal, standing like soldiers over their town.

Anna turned into a hidden drive in a grove of trees and the car crunched down a long unpaved road for several minutes. Eventually, they pulled over into a large clearing, and Keegan noticed Spencer's truck along with Calvron's red mustang. There were also several others that she didn't recognize.

"Where are we going?" Keegan asked as they stumbled down the rocks of a small hill. Anna and Lauren just laughed, not answering her as they came to the bottom. Keegan was entranced to find that, oddly, there was a wooden door standing seemingly on its own in the grass.

"Keegan, open the door!" Lauren practically yelled at her, shooing her towards the door.

Fascinated, Keegan peered around the wooden frame; nothing but more grass and woods behind it. She circled around it before turning back to her friends questioningly.

"Just open it," Anna giggled.

Grabbing the handle, Keegan yanked the door open.

What she saw left her speechless.

It looked like a magical wonderland. It was like stepping onto the page of a make-believe land in a novel or a movie. *Yeah, that's what it's like*: walking into the movie "Avatar." Everything was bright and cheerful. The plants and the flowers were lush and exotic, while the trees soared high over her head and the distant patter of rain on the canopy met her ears.

Lauren put her hands on Keegan's back and gave her a shove. "Yeah, yeah it's magical, just get in there."

Anna stepped through with Keegan, nudging

her shoulder, "I told you Calvron was amazing."

Keegan turned wide eyes to Anna, her mouth open. "He did this?"

"Yep," Anna nodded, her incredibly bright green eyes surveying the landscape. "He can create a whole alternate world. We come here to play and be ourselves." She gestured around them.

Keegan looked closer to where Anna had indicated and could see there were several different magical creatures already there with them. Of course, you couldn't miss the three huge, beautiful cats that sauntered their way. She laughed when they rubbed up against her legs as if they were pets. She could have sworn the tiger was purring. That would, of course, be Donald. She reached down and rubbed behind his ears, catching his big eyes with her own as he leaned his soft face into her hands.

Keegan watched Spencer in his panther form. His green eyes were shocking next to his black fur. Sam, even as a lion, was the most beautiful of the group. They nudged on Lauren and Anna playfully, trying to get them moving.

"One minute, let her take it all in, we don't have to start right away," Lauren chuckled, talking to Sam as she ran her hands through mane.

The big cats laid down and stretched out lazily, Spencer and Sam batting at each other with their giant paws. Lauren's wings unfurled behind her. Keegan reached out to touch one of the stars that danced around them, but her finger went right through it.

Glancing over at Anna, Keegan thought, *Wow.*

Both of her best friends were so beautiful, there was no doubt about that. Calvron's magical land only seemed to enhance their beauty, just like the flowers and the rest of their surroundings. Anna's eyes were always a startling color of green, but they were even more so here, almost a match for the vivid green color of the foliage. It was as if she were staring into emerald jewels instead of eyes. Everything about them was different. They almost looked like animated versions of themselves, their eyes larger and skin glowing.

Neither were in their regular clothes any longer, either. Lauren wore a sparkly dress that fell in pretty pink strips to her knees, while Anna wore a satiny, black sheath with bell sleeves.

Keegan couldn't help but wonder what she looked like. Too bad there wasn't a mirror around. She looked down, surprised to find that she wasn't in her jeans and t-shirt anymore. Her dress was an ankle length green affair with a form fitting bodice and a flowing skirt. She smiled.

They looked awesome.

Donald wasn't sure he could handle this.

Seeing Keegan always left him slightly in awe of her beauty, no matter where they happened to be. In this magical world with her beauty enhanced to its fullest potential, being near her was almost too much to bear.

He tried not to stare, really, but it was like he could sense her everywhere. Whenever he turned to find her, he couldn't help but get lost in her, only able to shake himself out of his daydreams when he realized she was looking back. He battled with himself not to watch her every move.

The excitement was clearly written all over her face. It was obviously hard for her to sit still as she flitted from flower to tree to rock, touching everything as she exclaimed over them. With the background of the forest and her auburn hair over that long, green dress, Donald thought she looked like a nymph of autumn. She was magnificent.

Slowly, Donald rose to all fours and gave his head a good shake. He circled around Keegan and wrapped his tail around her leg trying to tug her forward. A loud roar escaped from deep within him as he took off running. He could hear Keegan laughing as she chased after him down towards the water.

Submerging his powerful body under the water felt wonderful. It was the perfect temperature, like a warm bath. Eventually, Keegan made it to the edge of the lake, a little out of breath after chasing him. She had a mischievous grin on her face when she saw him in the water.

"Is it deep enough to dive?" Keegan yelled, her hands on her hips.

The tiger nodded his head yes, and she dove in, graceful as a dolphin. His heart was racing. Just the sight of her had such an effect on him.

She swam up to the tiger, her arms splashing gently through the water. "It's freezing."

"You're crazy. This water is warm," Donald answered, treading water with all four legs.

"Maybe when you're covered in fur, it's warm." Keegan stuck out her tongue, and then paused. "Hey, wait a minute! I didn't think you could speak?"

"In here we can pretty much do anything we want."

Keegan cocked her head at him, her hair plastered to her head in a way that was more endearing than unflattering. "I have to admit this is probably the most amazing place I have ever seen."

"Yeah, Calvron is something else. He can pretty much do anything. I can't imagine having that kind of power."

"Do you think he could bring the bond to my chosen back?"

Donald's whole body tensed. "No idea, why don't you ask him?" After a slight pause, he added, "Are you even sure you would want him to?"

Keegan stared at him like he was crazy. "Why wouldn't I want him to?"

"Well, don't you think it's a little strange that you are not comfortable around the person who is supposed to be your perfect match? Wouldn't you rather know that it was real and not just some magic bond that made you want to be with him?"

Her eyes on the large tiger before her, the water beading on his fur, Keegan realized had never thought of it that way. What if he was right? She would rather have true love than a magic spell that made them believe they were perfect together. Shouldn't she feel something for Rourk even if the bond was broken?

Ugh, it's all so confusing. She lay back in the water, her body floating as she put her head on the tiger. She was always so comfortable around Donald; too bad he wasn't interested in her more than a friend. "You know, you really are very

45

smart for a tiger."

He wasn't sure if it was the place that gave him the courage, or the fact that he was in his tiger form. Before he could stop the words, they spilled out. "I think you should give me a chance. What if we're perfect together *without* a bond?"

"Donald, stop joking around," Keegan said with a sigh, treading the water. "You already made it clear that you're not interested in me."

"That was before your bond was broken. Keegan, I've always been crazy about you. I just didn't want to get hurt. I knew you were an elf and that you were bound to another."

She stared across the expanse of water into the bright blue eyes of the talking tiger. *This is absurd*, she thought. *I'm talking to a tiger who wants to date me.*

Well, then why is your heart beating a mile a minute? she wondered. This did feel perfect. "Are you serious?"

"I have never been more serious about anything in my life. I know I joke around a lot..."

Keegan thought, *It is so weird to hear Donald's voice come from a tiger.* She giggled.

"This is not a laughing matter." The tiger cocked his head and glared. "Keegan, every time I see you I feel like I am on an elevator that has dropped. I think about you constantly. Maybe fate has stepped in and broken the bond so we can be together."

Keegan backed up enough to find the ground and stood. "I'm sorry, I need to think."

She disappeared before his eyes. Her main power

was invisibility; it was the first time he had seen her use it. Donald hoped he hadn't pushed her away. He couldn't imagine not having her in his life, even if she only wanted to be friends. Rolling over, he looked up at the sky. He had done all he could; it was up to her now.

Keegan was so confused and, oddly, a little angry. She tried to think positive thoughts to warm herself up as she trudged out of the water. Her dress and skin dried instantly; she guessed it was Calvron's magic that did it. Sitting down on a large, flat rock in the warm sunshine, she recalled the photos of her weekend with Rourk. They looked so happy together. Was she ready to give up on her chosen to give Donald a chance? Could she ever be that happy again without the bond?

She always knew there was something special about Donald. He was the only boy that kept her interest more than a couple of weeks. However, she really did need to think it over. Donald was a shape shifter and she was an elf. What if she fell in love with him and they got married? What would that mean for their children? She thought of her cousin, Keara. She was the only half elf that Keegan knew. Keara always felt so out of place among the rest of the elves. Did Keegan really want to do that to her own children? Ugh, she was ashamed of herself. She was a hypocrite. How many times had she sat down and told Keara how special she was for being different? And she truly meant it: Keara was amazing. She was obviously just looking for an excuse, an easy way out of this predicament.

What if she did lose her bond so she could

have a chance with Donald? Could she really turn her back on that?

The real question was could she turn her back on Rourk? He was her chosen after all.

Chapter 6

A voice shook her out of her thoughts. "Keegan, you're it. You could have picked a better hiding spot." Sam gave her a strange look, his blonde mane windblown from his romp through the woods. He was a magnificent lion, but she was still really fond of certain tiger.

She hadn't even noticed that she'd become visible again. "Hide and seek? Well, you guys are about to lose," Keegan answered, smirking as he roared and ran away.

Keegan leapt to her feet and took off running, deciding she would try playing the game without magic at first. She looked everywhere for several minutes, but could find no one. She was passing through a small clearing near a clear, trickling brook when she saw movement from the corner of her eyes. Wait, were those stars she had seen? She changed directions and headed towards a group of large, freestanding boulders. Yes, she saw them again. She closed her eyes and with her mind, she saw Lauren, her best friend, the fairy. Once again, Keegan was struck by her beauty. "Lauren, you're it."

Lauren came out from behind the huge boulder, putting her hands palm up as she shrugged. "I let you find me. I know you are not used to playing in the big leagues."

What the hell did that mean? Keegan wondered. Whatever, she would just disappear if anyone came close to catching her. She sprinted towards the forest searching for a great hiding spot. The trees were huge, their trunks the biggest she had ever seen. The colors were so vibrant it was mesmerizing.

Something compelled her to keep heading further into the woods. She kept going deeper into the shadows, the brush under her feet cracking, and she didn't want to stop. There was no way they would find her way back here.

She was sidetracked by the sound of whispers coming from the large hot pink flowers that lined the path upon which she walked. *Were they talking?* Keegan leaned down to put her ear next to the largest, and she heard Calvron's voice say, "You're it again." His laugh could be heard throughout the forest.

"Calvron, is that you? You're a flower?" Keegan was aghast. She poked one of the silky petals. The flower swayed back and forth a couple times, and vapor slowly appeared. It hid the flower and grew larger as Keegan stepped away from it.

In just a few seconds, Calvron was standing before her. He was a tall, lanky guy with shaggy dark blonde hair and pale blue eyes. Keegan had always thought he was kinda cute, but he was also too arrogant. "You really suck at this game, Keegan."

"What? How can you say that? You cheated!"

"I cheated? How is that?" He crossed his long arms over his chest. He looked rather outlandish, but somehow suave, in a pair of black cotton pants tucked into high leather boots, topped with his white cocktail jacket. The collar of a satiny shirt was open under his coat and there were white gloves on his hands.

"You were a flower."

"Keegan, this is the land of magic, of course magic will be used. Are you going to tell me you didn't think your little disappearing act would give you a leg up?"

She could feel the anger rising in her as coldness seeped through her body.

Calvron shook his head. "Keegan, you need to stop being a baby. I got you fair and square. You are no longer playing with a bunch of elves and humans. We all have powers here and we use them."

Hearing laughter, she glanced around to find there were at least twenty creatures of the light of different varieties staring and laughing at her. They popped out from behind trees and morphed from inanimate objects of the forest, just as Calvron had done from the flower. *How dare they!* They had some nerve making fun of her. Her fingernails dug into her palms. Suddenly, one by one they started disappearing and reappearing, blinking in and out of existence before her while their muffled laughter filled the air. Even Lauren and Anna were laughing.

"Elf, you're not so special in here," echoed through the forest.

Keegan was getting colder by the second, her lips quivering and her body shaking. A cracking sound startled her, like a gunshot through the woods, and when she looked down, the ground had turned to ice. The laugher had stopped.

Everyone had been turned to ice! *Oh my god, did I do this?*

A loud pop sounded, and the ice shattered around Calvron. He shook himself, brushing ice shards from the sleeves of his white jacket. His voice was serious when he asked, "Keegan, have you always had the ability to turn things to ice?"

She covered her mouth with her hand, her eyes wide. "No, this is the first time it has happened. I don't even know what I did."

"Well, it has to be a pretty strong power to work in this place," Calvron said softly, his jaw set in a hard line. "Negative or destructive magic is forbidden in here. What were you thinking when it happened?"

"I was angry that everyone was laughing at me."

"So, it's probably brought on by your temper. I don't recall you ever having a bad temper."

"I didn't, but since I was brought back to life, I seem to get angry easily and when I do, I get really cold. I can usually warm myself up by thinking positive thoughts. I guess this is the first time I've gotten so mad."

Calvron looked at her with interest. He had never come across something like this before; he loved puzzles.

Keegan returned his look with pleading eyes.

"Can you please help me?"

He paced around for several minutes as if he were deep in thought, intrigued by her newly revealed power. Finally, he came to a pause and shook his head at her, his hands clasped behind his back. "Keegan, I'm not sure I can. Whatever dark magic is in you is stronger than me. Not to brag or anything, but I'm pretty damn powerful. I will certainly look into it and see if there is anything I can do. The easiest thing is to try to avoid situations that make you angry."

She wanted to cry. *How could I have done this?* "Can't you at least unfreeze them?"

"Nope, that's on you. I was strong enough to break myself free. You need to figure out how to set them free."

"Calvron, this is *your* made up world. You fix it!" She yelled, watching in horror as the ice begin to cover him again. Hurriedly, she told him, "No, I'm sorry! I didn't mean it. Please stop. I'm not mad at you. You are one of my best friends. I know you would help me if you could."

The ice melted and Calvron was once again free, though wet.

Just then, Donald strolled up in tiger form, his tail flicking behind him. "What happened to them?" His big head jerked in the direction of the icy creatures.

"Why is he not frozen?" Keegan's voice sounded panicked.

"Hmm, if I had to guess it's because you weren't angry at him at the time." Calvron turned and explained to Donald what had happened.

Donald started intently at her. "Keegan, this is not who you are. Don't let your anger turn you into something you are not. You need to learn to control this. Before, you told me when you started to get cold you would think good thoughts to warm up. So, think of something that warms your heart."

She was still so angry that they had mocked her and laughed at her. Taking a deep breath, she tried to think of something that would make her happy. Why was she drawing a blank? It shouldn't be so hard.

Donald sprawled out next to her, using his back paw to scratch his ear. "I can still picture the first time I saw you and it always makes me smile."

Looking skeptical, Keegan responded, "You do?"

Laughing, he replied, "It was the first day of high school, and I believe it was in Latin class. The teacher was giving a long speech. She was going on and on about how we were freshman and had no idea what we were going to do with our lives. That we were scared and not sure of ourselves. Inside, we were all mentally agreeing. You raised your hand." The tiger laughed and shook his head. "The teacher called on you, and clear as can be you said, 'I'm going to be awesome.' I looked over at this auburn-haired beauty and couldn't help but laugh. I knew in that moment that I had to meet you. I needed to know who this girl with such unabashed confidence was."

She could feel her face flushing and a smile slowly crossed her face. The loud sound of ice cracking startled her. Looking around in relief, she saw all the creatures breaking free from the icy prison she had put on them. She felt light and happy. How was he able to have that affect on her so quickly? She was actually able to laugh at herself for getting angry over something as silly as a game of hide and seek.

"I do believe that's enough for today, everyone," Calvron called out. Right before her eyes the magical land was gone, and they all stood at the bottom of the hill below where the cars were parked. Donald, as well as the other creatures, were back in their human forms.

The door was gone.

Walking to his truck, Calvron yelled, "See you guys next week."

Keegan turned to Donald, "Thank you." She paused, started to talk, and stopped again.

"What is it, Keegan? You can tell me."

"It's just, I'm really scared, Donald. I'm glad you were there to help me fight through the darkness." She wrapped her arms tightly around herself and stared into his cerulean eyes.

"You will figure this out. There is so much good in you, the dark doesn't stand a chance. When you feel yourself getting angry, try to focus on something or someone that makes you smile."

Keegan looked down at her shoes and then back at Donald. "Thinking of you makes me smile."

Donald grinned and he quickly responded, "Would you like to go out with me sometime? Maybe we could go on a hike, or just hang out and watch a movie? "

"I think I would like that. Text me later and we'll make plans."

Keegan walked slowly over to Anna's car, her

mind racing. She was still so confused. However, she couldn't deny that she felt happiest when she was around Donald. Rourk was always in the back of her mind, but she still could not remember what if felt like to want to be with him.

Once she got to Anna's car, Anna started blasting out questions. "What happened? I feel like I lost time, but I have no idea why. All I remember is teasing you and next thing I know Calvron is telling everyone to go home." She looked down at her sweater. "What the heck is up with my clothes? They're wet!"

"So are mine," Lauren added from the backseat.

Sighing, Keegan told them about her temper leading them all to be frozen. How it seemed to be an unfortunate side affect of the dark magic.

Her friends' silence worried Keegan.

Glancing at Anna, Keegan saw the girl's jaw clenched. Keegan said, "I'm not mad at your mom, Anna."

Anna just nodded, her pink hair swishing. She didn't answer.

They drove to Lauren's house in silence. After they dropped her off, Keegan turned in her seat to look at Anna. "What do you think of Donald?"

"Well, that's an odd question." Anna's brow was furrowed when she glanced at Keegan. She turned her eyes back to the road. "I think he's a great friend. And he's hilarious."

"Do you think I should date him?"

Anna raised an eyebrow in her direction. "Where is this coming from? I know you used to have a crush on him, but I thought your focus was Rourk?"

"I feel nothing for Rourk," Keegan said, turning to look out the window. "There's just *nothing*. But when I'm around Donald, I feel happy and excited."

Anna stared at her friend, not sure what to say. Her mother's warning was ringing in her ears. "Well, you did used to date a lot before so I really don't think it's a big deal if you want to hang out with him."

"Yeah, that's what I was thinking too. I just don't want to hurt Rourk's feelings."

They drove the rest of the way home in silence. Anna needed to find the light witch quickly. Hopefully her mother had made some progress on her search.

After dropping Keegan off at home, Anna pulled out her cell and called her mother.

"Mom, have you found her yet?"

Her mother's sigh was weary. "Not yet, it's not as easy as you would think."

"Well, Keegan is already moving on from Rourk; she wants to date Donald."

"Anna, you have to let Keegan make her own choices. Don't try to talk her out of anything."

"As if that would be possible. Keegan is stubborn."

"Ok, well, I'll see you when you get home."

"Bye"

Anna was deep in thought. Sure, Keegan could probably be happy with Donald, but she deserved her chosen. Anna would do anything to know who her own perfect match was. Keegan had been handed hers, and then had it ripped away.

She had to figure out a way to get Keegan's bond back.

Chapter 7

Keegan walked through the door, energized from her time in Calvron's world and itching to share it with someone. Her mother was sitting in the living room with a book open on her lap, sipping a mug of something steamy.

"Hey, Mom!" Keegan said brightly.

Emerald looked up, one hand resting on the pages of her book, and smiled at her daughter. "Hey. Where have you been?"

"You will never believe! Calvron made this incredible magical land. We actually had to walk through a wooden door that was suspended in the air. It was amazing. I wish you could have seen it." Keegan's words rushed out quickly.

"Slow down, Keegan. Why don't you come sit down and tell me all about it?" She patted the seat beside her and turned to face Keegan.

Smiling, Keegan skipped over and sat beside her mom, chatting away as she described Calvron's world. After a while, she paused, biting her lip. She almost forgot to tell her about the freezing issue. "Mom, I learned of another side effect of the dark magic today."

"What?" Her mother gave her a concerned look, her blue eyes dark.

"Well, I have been noticing that when I get angry, I start to feel cold. Today, they were teasing me during a game and I got so mad that I froze them all on the spot...even the ground. Calvron and Donald were able to help me. When I think positive thoughts, the coldness goes away. So after Donald told me some stories that made me happy, the ice melted. I was really scared."

Her mother stared at Keegan without saying anything for several seconds. "Interesting," she finally murmured. "I guess it could be worse. You will just have to learn to keep your anger in check, Keegan. Believe me, I've been dealing with learning to control my temper most of my life. It is not an easy thing to do." The corners of her mouth turned down and her brow furrowed. She sighed, reaching to brush Keegan's hair behind one ear. "It is, of course, possible. Your father can work with you on breathing exercises. It also helps that you know how to keep it at bay through your thoughts and emotions. Obviously, trying to avoid situations that increase your anger is the easiest thing to do. Prevention is the best medicine, as they say. I just hope other side effects don't pop up." She put her arm around Keegan and gave her a squeeze.

"Mom, I think I like Donald." Keegan spit out before she gave it too much thought. She really wanted her mother's thoughts on it.

"What do you mean you think you like him?"

Emerald asked, pulling away to catch her daughter's eyes. "As in more than a friend?"

"Yes. He makes me happy. I feel special when he is around." Her cheeks flushed as she looked down to where her hands were clasped in her lap.

"Keegan, you've met your chosen. You cannot be interested in others."

"Mother, I can't even remember Rourk. He's literally a stranger to me," Keegan said softly, rubbing her arms in an attempt to warm herself up.

Reaching over her daughter, Emerald pulled a throw blanket from the back of the couch and handed it to Keegan. "You really should give Rourk a chance, Keegan. But, if you are interested in Donald then perhaps you should see where it goes. I do suggest that you take it slow. I don't have to remind you that elves are supposed to partner with elves. You *have* been dating humans for years so I guess dating a shape shifter is not the end of the world." Emerald gave her a wry smile.

Keegan reached over and hugged her mother. "Thank you for understanding."

Slowly, Keegan headed up the stairs to her room, the blanket still draped tightly around her shoulders. She was actually pretty sad at the thought of moving on from Rourk. How many hours had she sat around daydreaming about meeting her chosen and their perfect life? He was incredibly cute, too.

Her phone vibrated and she looked down to see it was a text from Donald.

Night beautiful.

Smiling she replied back. *Night and you're*

not so bad yourself.

A goofy grin spread across her face as she changed into her pajamas and crawled into bed, adding the blanket from downstairs on top of her comforter for extra warmth. She was excited to see Donald at school tomorrow.

When she rolled out of bed the next morning and looked at the clock, Keegan noticed she had better hurry up unless she wanted to be late again. At least she had her Jeep now so she could speed if needed. Of course, she couldn't find her sweater. She misplaced at least one piece of her school uniform everyday.

"Mom, where's my sweater?" Keegan yelled out her bedroom door, tearing through the pile of clothes in her desk chair.

"Did you look in your closet?" her mother called back, her voice thin and reedy from down the hall.

"Ugh, of course I did!"

Her mom's footsteps sounded down the hall and she walked in, moved a couple of things around, and pulled the sweater off the back of the chair.

"I looked there."

Raising an ironic eyebrow, Emerald replied, "Obviously."

Keegan rushed out of the house a few minutes later. She still had enough time to make it to school before the bell rang. She wanted to get there a little early to see Donald.

She pulled into the lot of school after breaking several speed limits to get there and went inside. As she was walking down the hall, one of the teachers yelled out, "Keegan, your sweater is inside out."

Looking down, Keegan saw the little tag hanging from the inside seam at her waist. She shrugged and waved to the teacher where he was grinning outside his classroom. "Thanks."

Where is he? she thought as she scanned the halls. She didn't see Donald anywhere. Spencer and Sam were deep in conversation, so she didn't want to bother them to ask.

Lauren and Anna were waiting at her locker. "Hey, guys."

"Keegan, your hair is a mess. Get over here so I can fix it," Lauren said with a puzzled look.

Keegan ran her hand over her hair and realized she hadn't even brushed it. It was official; she was going mad.

"Just put this clip in it and it'll be fine." Anna reached into her big purse and pulled out a clip with a huge blue flower on it, passing it to Lauren.

"Let's hope there are no bees in here 'cause I'll surely be attacked" Keegan joked.

"You're just *so* funny, Keegan." Lauren rolled her eyes, adjusting the clip in Keegan's hair. "You'll see. It's actually really cute."

"If you say so."

"Voila!" Lauren dramatically moved her hands as if Keegan was a piece of art on display.

Keegan glanced in her locker mirror, turning her head from side to side. "It *is* kinda cute."

The warning bell rang. Keegan waved to her friends as they all ran off in separate directions to their classrooms.

She was bummed she didn't get to see Donald.

The morning seemed to drag on. Donald was nowhere to be found between classes and she started to wonder if he was avoiding her. It didn't make any sense, though, because she hadn't done anything wrong. Maybe he was sick? Hopefully she would find out at lunch.

She was relieved to see a flash of orange hair when she entered the cafeteria. Her pulse quickened as he walked towards her.

"Hey Keegan, nice flower."

She self-consciously touched her hair. "Thanks, I think. I thought you might be sick or something. I haven't seen you all morning."

"Nah, I just woke up late. Let's go grab something to eat."

"Umm, sure." He had never asked her to eat lunch with him before. She wanted to run over and tell Anna and Lauren, but that would be silly. They would figure out it out on their own.

Keegan grabbed a hamburger, fries, and some chocolate milk. She hesitated and then grabbed a slice of cake.

"You eat a lot for a girl."

"I hear that all the time. One of the perks of having pointy ears is I have a high metabolism."

"Yeah, same for me. No matter how much I eat, I can't seem to keep on any real weight."

She looked him up and down. "You look fine to me."

"Well, thank you." His face was bright red, making his blue eyes seem even brighter.

Keegan had an odd urge to reach up and kiss him. *Sure, great idea in the middle of the cafeteria.*

"Are we going to sit with the guys?"

"Nope, I want you all to myself today. If that's

okay with you?"

"Of course it is." Keegan smiled up at him.

Keegan couldn't believe this was happening. After all this time, Donald was into her.

Her tray went flying as she tripped and started to fall. Luckily, she caught herself on the corner of a nearby table as she fell. *What the heck! What did I trip over?* Well, if people hadn't noticed them together before, they did now. The kids at the tables around them were snickering as Keegan tried to clean up the mess.

"Keegan, it's no big deal. I'll go grab you another tray of food." Donald set his tray on the table. "You look super cute when you're clumsy." He winked at her and walked off.

Keegan found herself smiling as she picked up the splattered cake. Donald seemed to have a knack for defusing situations.

He came back with a tray that had twice as much food as the last. "We can't have you hungry with the big chemistry test at the end of the day."

"Thanks." Keegan looked around to see if anyone was staring at her. Everyone had gone back to eating and chatting, oblivious to the two of them.

"Are you ready for the test?" he asked her as they took seats across from each other at an empty table.

"Sure. I don't have to study for science and math." Keegan shrugged and shoved a fry in her mouth.

"Must be nice," Donald laughed, pulling the top bun off of his hamburger before ripping open a packet of ketchup. "I have to study a lot. My mom would kill me if I got bad grades."

They were silent as she finished off her fries and watched him pile his burger high with vegetables and condiments.

He took a bite and seemed to barely chew it before swallowing. "Keegan, do you want to go for a bike ride with me on Saturday? I'd like to show you one of my favorite places."

"I would love that. I'm not a very good at it so I hope you don't need me to go mountain biking." Keegan made a face at him then took a drink of her milk.

"Well, it *is* in the woods, but we can hike from the road."

"I can't wait! Do you want me to bring lunch for us?"

"Leave it to you to think of food." He chuckled, shaking his head. "Of course, that would be great, we could make a day out of it."

She tried to be nonchalant about it, but inside she was dancing and jumping around. *Donald asked me out!*

Chapter 8

Keegan was super excited. Today was her first date with Donald; they were going for a hike and picnic. She looked around her room trying to think of what to wear. It was starting to get cool out so she knew she should dress warm. Of course, she still had to look cute.

Keegan sent Lauren a text: *What should I wear on a hiking date?*

With your chosen? :)

No, with Donald.

What!?? When did this happen, and why am I just finding out about it?

I'll fill you in later, what should I wear?

I hope you know what you are doing. Wear your new black skinny jeans and that teal tight sweater to show off your curves.

Oooh great choice! What would I do without you?

Uh huh. Let me know how it goes. Donald? I still can't believe it.

Keegan got dressed and ran down the stairs, jumping the last two with a grin.

"Where are you off to all excited?" Her mother asked with a smile. She was tapping away at the keyboard of her Macbook.

"I have a date with Donald. Can you throw me together a picnic lunch?"

The smile faded. "Keegan, so soon? Don't you think you should give Rourk more time?"

"It's just a hike, Mom, don't worry." Keegan opened the fridge and pulled out a couple of drinks. "What should I bring for food?"

"Well, I would have needed more notice for something fancier, so you're stuck with sandwiches and chips." Leaving her computer with a sigh, her mother opened the bread box and pulled out the loaf.

"That works. Make us both two sandwiches. I'm really hungry."

"Aren't you always?" Her mother threw together the sandwiches and sealed them up, and then grabbed some chips and threw them in a bag. "Here ya go. I hope you aren't gone all day. Your room is a mess."

Keegan rolled her eyes. "I'll see you when I get back." She blew her mom a kiss and slammed the door behind her.

Donald didn't have his own car so she drove over to pick him up. She blared her radio, and sang along to the latest Lady Gaga, tapping her fingers on the steering wheel. As soon as she pulled in, Donald sauntered out, his hands in his pockets.

Keegan's heart fluttered as he slid into the passenger seat and closed the door. She smiled.

"So, where do you want to go hiking? I guess we're skipping the bike ride?"

"You'll see. It's my special spot. I've actually never taken anyone there."

Keegan grinned. "Really? Not even the guys?"

"No one. I like to go there and think sometimes or just be alone."

"I have a spot like that, too. It's my favorite place to take photos." Keegan slammed her hand on the steering wheel. "Shoot, I forgot my camera."

"No biggie, you can bring it next time." He pulled his cap a little lower and gave her a lopsided grin that made her heart flutter.

Keegan followed his directions until he prompted her to turn into a hidden driveway. They parked in an empty field, jumped out, and grabbed their lunch.

It was a long hike and Keegan quickly became tired. "Are we almost there?"

"Yep, just about five more minutes."

Donald grabbed her hand and pulled her up the last bit of the hill. They crested the top, and Keegan stared out over the scenery, wide-eyed. "Wow, it's amazing." She looked down over the cliff at the assortment of colors from the leaves changing. "I feel so small up here." She whispered. "I really wish I had my camera."

Rourk was out on his daily trek in the woods trying to enjoy what was left of fall before winter took over. He still hiked in the winter, it just wasn't as enjoyable. He stopped in his tracks and listened intently. He could hear someone talking, which was odd since he couldn't remember the last time he saw anyone in this part of the woods. It was very secluded.

He heard laughter and his heart dropped. He must be losing his mind. He could have sworn that it sounded just like Keegan's laugh. But what would she be doing way up here? Rourk silently went in the direction of the voices, careful not to make a sound so he didn't startle anyone. He wanted to prove to himself he wasn't going crazy.

As he got closer, he stopped dead in his tracks. His heart rate skyrocketed. It was Keegan, and she was there with the shapeshifter. Rourk clenched his fist and closed his eyes, trying to compose himself. He opened his eyes and stood eerily still, watching the two. He had to will himself to stay in place. He felt like a cave man— he wanted to throw her over his shoulder and drag her away from the cat. He knew he couldn't do that. He should turn and leave; it was as if he was frozen in place.

He watched as Keegan smiled up at the shifter and played with her hair. He cringed when she leaned over to wipe something off his face. Rourk could feel the rage building in him. He didn't know how to bring it down.

He's so cute. Keegan thought, smiling as she wiped mustard from the side of his mouth. His skin was warm even though the air was cool.

Donald lightly wrapped his hand around her wrist as she touched his face and pulled her towards him. Keegan's heart pounded. She reached up and wrapped her hands around his neck to pull him forward. As she leaned down, her head hit the bill of his cap. She giggled, embarrassed, and pulled back. "I'm sorry. I don't know what came over me," she gasped, her face flushed as she looked down at her hands.

Donald chuckled, and threw his cap to the side. His bright blue eyes were such a contrast to his pale skin and orange hair as he stared at her. "Come here."

She let his arms encircle her waist, his hands were hot even through her shirt as scooted closer to him.

Keegan's pulse quickened as he leaned down and kissed her. This time their lips met his, and their kiss was soft and light. Keegan pulled him a little closer causing him to intensify the kiss.

Suddenly Keegan pulled back looking around nervously. "Did you hear that?"

"It was probably just a deer." Donald smiled and pulled her back into him.

Chapter 9

Rourk decided to check up on Keegan. Seeing her kiss the tiger on Saturday had nearly destroyed him, but he'd managed to convince himself she was living in the moment. He had felt unbearable jealousy when he found them together in the woods, but had managed to escape back into the wilderness before they saw him. He longed for a hint from her that she still cared for him. Anything, really.

He closed his eyes and of course, that didn't work. All he saw was darkness. His hands clenched into fists. He hated feeling so helpless.

Keegan hadn't contacted him since their date. He didn't want to put pressure on her because he knew she needed her space, but it was just so hard to sit back and do nothing, especially when he knew Donald was having success where he'd failed. He wished someone could find a way to bring back their bond. He was obviously doing a poor job of winning her over on his own.

They weren't even supposed to meet until she turned eighteen, anyway, so he had to remind himself to just be patient. He had been given a gift in being able to be with her before their time.

He knew he shouldn't do it, but he couldn't help himself. He closed his eyes and thought of Lauren, and as he suspected, Keegan was with her. She was laughing at something, which brought a smile to Rourk's face. He wished his ability allowed him to hear what was being said and to hear her laughter.

He watched as Keegan jumped up from her chair and ran over to the orange-haired boy. She looked so excited. It was like a knife driven into Rourk's heart. He opened his eyes; he couldn't watch any longer.

Grabbing his pack, he decided to go on a long hike to clear his head.

He felt at home in the woods. He was grateful to have work to keep him busy. At least all the training kept his mind occupied and gave him a reprieve from his thoughts of Keegan.

Rourk couldn't help himself; eventually he checked in on Lauren again. Keegan was still there, and she seemed to be hanging on to every word the shapeshifter said. He wished he wasn't capable of feeling the jealousy he felt. On an impulse, he pulled out his phone and sent her a text. As he hit send, he closed his eyes to see her reaction.

He watched as she looked down at her phone and put it back in her purse without replying, turning back to the other boy. Rourk's eyes snapped opened, his heart racing. She really felt nothing for him.

It was starting to feel as if he didn't stand a chance of winning her back. Maybe he should just leave her alone until she turned eighteen. After all, it was one of the elfin rules. She was obviously not interested in him. He didn't exactly have skills in the romantic field. Perhaps if he let her obvious crush on the boy run its course, she would be ready to give him a shot later on. It really wasn't fair to her to make her choose. He was quite sure if he asked her to pick he would lose, and he couldn't handle that right now.

Rourk finished his hike and headed back home. After taking a quick shower, he grabbed a sandwich and read for a little while, trying to banish the memory of Keegan's lips touching the shapeshifter's. Finally, sleep washed over him

He woke with a start some time later and knew what he had to do. Throwing on a pair of jeans and a t-shirt, he grabbed the keys to his truck and headed out the door.

He wasn't quite sure where he was going, so he looked it up on his GPS. The drive wasn't long and he didn't allow himself to think too much. He was afraid he would change his mind.

It was nothing special. A single glass door and picture window in a strip mall near the center of town. The bell went off as he strode into the room. Without even bothering to look around, he walked straight to the man behind the desk.

"I'm here to enlist. I will be joining the 18X program." Rourk stated in a clear, concise manor.

The sergeant looked up from his paperwork with a smirk on his face. "Is that so? You think you can just waltz in here and tell us what you want to do? You think you can walk in here and tell me you are going to try out for the Special Forces off the street?"

"Actually, I know I can. I am more than qualified. Of course, I will have to jump through hoops and take your assessments. I have no doubt I can pass anything you throw at me with flying colors."

The sergeant stared at him in silence for a moment as if he were studying him. He leaned back in the cheap office chair and tapped his pen on the desk. "Normally, I would kick a punk out for coming in and acting all arrogant in my office. However, you don't really sound arrogant. You might as well have stated the sky was blue."

Rourk met his gaze and remained expressionless.

"What is your name son?"

"Rourk."

"Rourk, do you have a last name?"

"My last name is Kavanagh."

"Rourk Kavanagh, how old are you?"

"I'm 18."

"Do your parents know you are here?"

"No, but it has been expected. My family has always known I would be a soldier, following in my father's footsteps."

"So your father was in the Army?"

"Actually, he was a Marine Recon."

This brought a loud laugh form the recruiter. "You don't think he will mind his son joining the Army?"

"No, he will understand my reasons. Currently the Army is the only service with the option to go straight into special operations. Now, if I told him I had joined the Air Force, he might have issues."

The sergeant laughed loudly. "What is your father's name?"

"Greg Kavanagh"

The recruiter quickly typed the name in the computer. Scanning quickly through the files, he finally said, "It seems as if your father had quite the career. Almost everything is classified."

Rourk looked him in the eyes but said nothing.

"Did he prepare you as you were growing up?"

"You could say that."

The recruiter slapped his hands to the desk as he stood. "Ok, Rourk, I have to say you have piqued my interest. Let's see how well you can 'jump through the hoops'. First, you are going to have to take the ASVAB, and a PT test, and we will go from there."

"I would like to leave ASAP. The faster we can get this over with, the better it will be. I would like to leave for basic before the month is out."

The recruiter stared at him. Finally, his lips twitched as if trying to hide a smile. "Go in the back room and they will proctor your ASVAB. The results will be almost instant because it's all done through the computer now."

Rourk nodded his head towards the recruiter and walked to the back of the room. The test was a joke. He finished and walked back to the recruiter's desk.

The sergeant looked at his watch. "You're already finished?"

"Yes."

"I'll be right back."

Rourk could see him talking to the woman in the office. He seemed agitated as he walked back towards his desk. "Rourk, would you mind taking another test?"

"I'll do whatever is required."

After the second round, the recruiter made a phone call. "Sir, we have a young man in here that just aced the ASVAB in record time." After a slight pause "Yes, I made him take another version. The same result. No, he is not interested in any of those fields. He wants to join the 18X program." He listened some more and after the call was ended, he looked at Rourk as if he was trying to understand him.

"I can't change your mind can I? How about the intelligence field?"

"No, 18X or nothing."

"Well, let's get the PT test over with. I'm sure that won't be an issue for you."

After scoring a perfect score of 300 on the PT test, the recruiter asked if Rourk would go to the range with him. The recruiter explained this was not something that was normally done. However, he was interested and wanted to see with his own eyes if Rourk would live up to the expectations that had formed in the recruiter's head.

Rourk loved shooting, so it was fun for him.

The recruiter shook his head when he looked at the dime sized hole in the target paper. "Very impressive. The Army will be proud to have you as one of their own. We have a group shipping out to basic on Friday if you are serious about wanting to go right away."

"Thank you. I will be ready."

The recruiter shook his hand. "I'm going to

keep my eye out for you, son. I think you will make quite the name for yourself."

Rourk shook his head roughly. "I'd rather remain anonymous."

"Too late for that. The instructors will easily pick you out. Soldiers like you will always stand out. They will try to break you. For the record, my money is on you."

Rourk grabbed all the info he needed and headed back to his house.

It was going to be so hard to leave Keegan. He only had three days before he left. He wasn't sure if he should see her or just make a clean break. She deserved the chance to be happy.

He knew it wouldn't do any good but he tried anyway. Closing his eyes, all he saw was darkness. It killed him that he could no longer see her or sense when she thought his name. He wondered what she was doing right now. She was probably with the tiger. Just thinking about it made him clench his jaw.

Once in his room back home, he sat at his desk and wrote her a letter. He folded the paper and put it in an envelope; he would leave it in her mailbox on his way to the airport.

Now, he had to tell his father.

Rourk walked into the living room and sat across from his dad. "I will be leaving on Friday. I am joining the U.S Army and going through the 18X program."

His father glanced up, mouth set in a grim line. "I think that is a wise decision. Have you told Richard?"

"No, I will inform him tomorrow at work."

"What about Keegan?"

"I wrote her a letter."

"Are you sure you don't want to tell her in person?"

He hesitated for only a second. "I can't handle that right now."

"I understand." His father clasped his hand on Rourk's shoulder with nothing more to say.

Rourk stood up and headed back to his room. He went over his packing list and started preparing to leave.

Early the next morning he found Richard and asked if they could speak in private. Richard led him to his office and gestured for him to sit down.

He was a large man, made even more impressive by his thick head of bright red hair and bushy beard. Rourk was impressed by the man's collection of visible scars, wounds from previous battles. He looked up to his commander.

"Richard, I am leaving on Friday. I have decided to go ahead with my plan of joining the U.S military."

"I see. Are you sure this is the route you should be taking?"

"I believe it is the right thing to do," Rourk said diplomatically. "I would love nothing more than to stay here and be with your daughter. After careful thought, I have realized the only thing I can do is leave. She deserves the time and space. We were brought together before we were meant to be. She should be able to enjoy her last year of high school without worrying about me. I will return when she is eighteen and we can decide where to go from there."

Richard peered intently at him, his arms crossed on the surface of his desk. "I don't have to tell you that the training will take a couple of years."

"No, you don't. I'm well aware of the schedule. I have been planning this since I was a young boy. Until you gave me the opportunity to stay on with the Army of the Light, this was always the plan. We strayed from the plan by allowing me to meet Keegan early, and that didn't go over so well. I think it's time I get back on course."

"Valid arguments. They will be lucky to have you. It is an experience that you will learn and grow from. Do you know where you want to go? Will you try to stay close by and opt for 5th Special Forces Group? Your Arabic is well above the requirements."

"Actually, I have been brushing up on Chinese since I learned Keegan's dream was to go to college in Alaska. That would allow me to be in Washington state which is the closest I can get to Alaska."

"Very well, you have obviously thought this through. It saddens me to see you go. You are an exemplary soldier."

"Thank you for putting your faith in me. I hope someday I can be half the warrior you are."

Standing up, Richard patted him on the shoulder, "You already are, son."

Rourk walked out of Richard's office and into the camp. Glancing around, he realized he had no one else to tell. He had always been a loner. Even so, he would miss this place; it was like a second home to him. But, he was determined. He strode off without looking back.

Chapter 10

Keegan pushed through the door and threw her backpack on the floor. She was glad it was Friday. She was looking forward to a break from school. Hopefully, they were going to be able to go back to Calvron's magical land over the weekend. It had been on her mind all week.

Walking into the kitchen, she saw a note propped up on the kitchen counter. It had her name written on it in neat block letters. Curious, she opened it and read

Keegan,
When you read this letter I will be on my way to basic training. I have decided to go ahead with my life-long plan. I will join the human military like the elves before me. I know I have been offered a position in the Army of the Light, however, I feel it is best I leave and continue with the path that was set from the day I was born. We shouldn't have even met yet. You should be enjoying your high

school years and having the time of your life with your friends. When you turn eighteen, I will come back for you. Perhaps you will have found a way to get our bond back. If you have not, and you wish me to let you go, I will do so. Just know Keegan, you are the only one for me. I will wait forever. Leaving you is the hardest thing I have ever had to do. Not a day will pass that I will not think of you. Every night when I close my eyes I will hope that by some miracle I can see you with my mind's eye again. Even if you decide you do not wish to be with me when you are of age, I will be forever grateful to you. The short time I spent with you were the happiest moments of my life.

Forever Yours, Rourk

Keegan reread the letter three times. She wasn't sure what to think. She felt sad that he was gone. She was also really annoyed that he didn't try harder to win her over. The more she thought about it, the angrier she got. The paper turned to a sheet of ice in her hands. Keegan dropped the note on the counter and pulled her sweater tighter. Why was she so angry? She should be relieved. Now she could date Donald and not worry about hurting Rourk's feelings. For some reason, that thought didn't bring her much comfort.

Thaddeus came downstairs, took one look at his sister sitting in a chair at the kitchen table, and asked, "What's the matter?"

Keegan gestured down at the paper which was now in a puddle of water at her feet. Leaning to pick it up, she shook the water off of it and thrust the soggy note into her brother's chest. "Let me guess, you didn't see this coming?"

He grabbed the letter and read it. As he was reading, he had flashes of a vision. *Rourk was in uniform with a look of indifference on his face, getting screamed at by an instructor. Rourk lying on his cot looking at the ceiling. The tiger in the woods. Anna holding a ruby ring in her hand.*

His visions drove him crazy. What did Anna have to do with all of this and why were they showing him a ruby ring? It was pretty obvious why Rourk and the tiger were in the vision. Leave it to Keegan to create a love triangle between an elf and a shape shifter.

Thaddeus mentally scanned books he had read, looking for rings. He could have smacked himself in the head when it finally dawned on him. How could he have missed something so simple?

Thaddeus handed the note back to Keegan. "I can't say I blame him for leaving. Probably a smart move on his part."

"Thaddeus, please tell me." Keegan pleaded, reaching up to tug on her brother's black t-shirt. "Am I going to get my bond back with Rourk?"

"Keegan, I couldn't tell you even if I knew, which I don't." Thaddeus gave her a look of pity. "I haven't had any visions of you since you came back from the dead. You are closed off from me as well."

Keegan walked across the room and plopped down on the couch like the drama queen she was. "This sucks!"

"Keegan, do you want your bond back with Rourk?" Thaddeus asked, following behind her to stand next to the arm of the couch.

"I don't know. I'm an elf. I'm supposed to be bonded to my chosen. It's what I've always expected. It's really not fair." She crossed her arms over her chest with a pout and leaned her head back on the couch.

"It could be worse. You could be dead," Thaddeus reminded her.

"Ugh!" Keegan groaned, whipping a pillow from the couch beside her and throwing it at him.

Thaddeus dodged it with a chuckle. "How's Anna?"

Keegan looked up at her brother, narrowing her eyes suspiciously. "Since when do you care about my friends?"

"I don't know. I was just curious as to how she took finding out about her mother and the black magic. Did she already know about it?" He needed to find a way to get Anna alone so they could talk.

Keegan sat up. She loved to gossip. "She had NO idea, and she was quite upset with her mother. It seems her mom has not helped her at all with her gift."

"What's her gift?"

Keegan looked taken aback. She always expected him to know everything before she did. "I thought you knew. She's a light witch."

Interesting, maybe there is hope after all.

"Thaddeus, you should come with us this weekend to the magical world that Calvron created, it's amazing. You could probably bring Sam."

Distracted, he said, "Sure, sounds like fun."

"Can't you do something about this whole frozen thing I have going on?"

"No, I can't. Just stop getting angry over stupid things."

"Easy for you to say." Keegan kicked her legs up on the table and glared at her brother.

"I'm going for a run." He walked out without looking at her.

About twenty minutes later, Keegan's mother came through the door with a couple of reusable grocery bags in her hands. Keegan peeked out of the blanket she was wrapped in.

"What's wrong, Keegan?"

"Rourk left." A hint of sadness was in her voice.

"What do you mean he left?" Emerald asked, walking past Keegan on her way to the kitchen to deposit her bags on the table.

"He's gone off and joined the military. The human military." Pulling the blankets closer to her chest, Keegan sat up and crossed her legs, staring at her mother.

"Did he come by to tell you?" her mother asked. She took off her green North Face jacket and hung it on the peg by the back door.

"Nope, he left me a note." She nodded towards the table.

"Can I read it?"

"Sure, why not."

Keegan watched as her mother read through the note. Her expression gave nothing away.

Finally, Emerald laid the paper on the table and glanced over at her daughter. "Keegan, this is a very sweet letter. You must realize how hard this was for him. I know you can no longer feel the bond to him. However, for him it's as strong as ever. To walk away from your chosen is no easy feat. He obviously cares deeply about you."

"What do you think I should do?" Keegan hadn't meant for her voice to sound so small.

"That's up to you. I think Rourk is very wise. He realizes you need your space to figure this out. You did meet before your time. I think this is for the best. Enjoy your time with your friends just as you did before you met him."

"I wish I remembered him, Mom."

"I know, sweetie. I wish you did too."

In the silence that followed, Keegan and her mother felt Richard arrive home at the same time and said simultaneously, "Dad's home." They laughed.

A few moments later, Keegan's father came through the door with, of all people, Creed. Keegan wasn't sure she'd ever get used to seeing them together. The leader of the light and the leader of the dark working together, friends even. It shocked everyone involved.

Her father walked over and kissed her mom. "How was your day?"

Her mother smiled up at her father. "Better now."

Richard grinned like a fool. It was almost sickening to see elf couples together. Ugh, she was supposed to have that with Rourk. Keegan wanted to cry.

"Did you know Rourk has left and joined the human military?" Keegan blurted out.

"Yes, he came and talked to me," Richard answered, stroking his red beard and not quite meeting her eyes. "He's just trying to do what's best for you, Keegan. Joining the human army is a long tradition for elves. I think it's the right thing for him to do."

Neither Keegan nor her mother said anything.

Richard addressed his wife. "Creed and I are going to be going out of town for a few days. We have some business to take care of."

"Saving the humans from destruction one day at a time?" Keegan rolled her eyes and cuddled back down under her blanket.

Her father ruffled her hair. "Something like that kiddo."

"Will you two be staying for dinner?" her mother asked.

Richard exchanged a glance with Creed, who had been respectfully silent during the scene. The leader of the dark grinned. "I can't speak for Richard, but I'm starving. I'd love to stay for dinner."

Emerald smiled and headed off to the kitchen.

"You might have made a mistake, Creed," Keegan said, shaking her head sadly. "My mom isn't much of a cook."

Her father chuckled. "Keegan, that's not true. Your mom is a great cook."

Her mother peeked around the corner. "I can hear you guys."

Keegan sat up straighter. "Creed, when you get angry do you turn things into ice?"

Creed laughed. "I can't say that I have that ability. Why do you ask?"

Keegan sunk back into the couch. "That's what happens to me. When I get angry my body starts getting cold and when I get *really* angry, I freeze everyone around me. I thought maybe it was a dark thing since you guys always have a lower body temperature."

"Why am I just hearing about this now?" Her father stared intently at her.

"I don't know, Dad, why am I just hearing about Rourk leaving?"

"Fair enough."

Creed was watching her from across the room. "I have to say that is very interesting, Keegan. I will ask around, maybe someone can help from the side of the dark."

"That would be great. I don't need to attract attention to myself by randomly freezing people."

They chatted for a while and then had dinner. Emerald had made chicken breast, rice, and corn and it was surprisingly good. Thaddeus still hadn't returned from his run. He could spend all day out in the woods.

Her father and Creed left, and Keegan sat at the table with her mom having a cup of hot tea.

"Mom, you don't mind Dad being gone all the time? That's what it would be like for me if I stayed with Rourk. I'm not sure I would like it too much."

Her mother looked over and smiled. "I don't think I could handle it if your father was home all the time. I like having my space. Plus, it makes us miss each other more."

"I can see that, I guess." Leaning back she crossed her arms like a spoiled toddler about to stomp her feet. "Mom, what am I going to do? This is so confusing for me."

"It will all workout. Life is funny. You don't always take the path you expected to take." Emerald stood, her mug in hand. "I need to make some phone calls. If you need to talk later, you know where to find me."

After her mother left, Keegan flipped through the TV channels. Nothing good was on. There were so many crappy shows out. She really didn't get the interest. Too bad *Vampire Diaries* wasn't on, now that was a good show. There was never enough Damon Salvator.

Looking down at her phone, she realized she had never replied to Rourk's text. She quickly typed. *Sorry I didn't reply earlier I was at school. I got your letter.*

Keegan waited for a reply, but it never came.

Touching her lips she thought of the kiss with Donald. She was so confused. She really liked Donald, but she also felt sad about Rourk leaving. *Why did things have to get so complicated?*

She felt like she was about to go stir crazy staying in the house. She went up to her room to go through some photos. Editing usually kept her mind busy.

On an impulse, she looked through the photos of her and Rourk. She did this at random times hoping it would bring back some feelings. Sadly, it did not.

After a couple of hours of manipulating photos, she got ready to go to sleep. She pulled her covers over her head and fell back on the bed. She wasn't tired. She would probably be up all night going over everything in her head. It was ironic that saving Donald severed her bond to her chosen. Maybe fate really had stepped in.

Her phone beeped, bringing a smile to her face. It was Donald.

Goodnight, I can't wait to see you tomorrow.
Ditto, sleep well.

Chapter 11

It was early morning when Rourk walked through the doors at the Military Entrance Processing Station. Glancing around, he saw many young guys and girls that appeared nervous and unprepared. The building was sterile and drab. The grey walls with the peeling paint reminded him of a prison. In a way, it was.

They were all at the MEPS to sign away a few years of their lives.

After signing in, Rourk waited his turn for the medical exam which he passed with flying colors. He already had an 18X slot, so he got to bypass some of the steps. However, it was still a lot of the "Hurry up and wait" for which the Army is famous.

Rourk could have laughed when he was brought into a room and taught how to stand at attention. They obviously didn't know he'd been going through the motions for several years already. He knew he had more experience than the others, but he just sat back and did what was asked of him, regardless of expertise.

A young officer went over the Oath of Enlistment with him. Apparently, they were afraid someone might stand incorrectly or not repeat the correct words. It was a joke. After they thought he was fully prepared, they sent him to sign his contract and take the oath. They seemed surprised that he didn't have any family members there to take his photograph. Whatever.

It turned out to be a long day, but rather painless. As he walked out the door and felt the crisp air hit him, he thought about Keegan. He wondered what she was doing and if she was angry at him for not seeing her before he left. Hopefully, he had made the right decision, because he would not see her again for almost a year. Just the thought of it made physical pain shoot through his body.

Grabbing a taxi to his run-down hotel, he forced himself to move forward. He could do this. He was doing this for her. If his unhappiness is what it took for her to be happy, he would endure the pain.

Rourk walked in the door of the hotel for which the military was paying, and the smell of mildew and cigarette smoke hit him. *Great. Oh well, it could always be worse.* He hung the *do not disturb* sign and locked the door. Rourk tossed his bag on the stained chair and headed for the shower.

The water pressure was pathetic, but at least the water was hot. He turned it on as hot as it would go and just stood there with his eyes closed. Finally, he washed up and got out, drying off before he walked back out to the room. He wasn't tired, but knew he would need his sleep.

He lay in bed and replayed scenes in his mind of Keegan. Her laugh, the way she skipped all over the place, her eyes that he could stare into forever, her hair that was almost always a mess, the way she kissed. He had to stop himself before he drove himself crazy.

He took some deep breaths and cleared his mind. Every time she crept back into his mind he pushed it away. After hours of fighting it, he drifted off to sleep.

Yelling woke him up. He looked at his watch; it was 3am. *That's what you get when you stay at a cheap hotel in the ghetto.* He didn't even bother to pay attention to the argument. It was none of his business. He might as well get up. The bus would be there at 4:00 to take them to Fort Benning, Georgia. After he did his morning workout, changed clothes, and ate a protein bar, he strolled out to wait for the bus.

There were a few others already waiting. He looked over the recruits, and they mostly looked tired. One young kid was pacing around, obviously nervous.

About twenty minutes later, a bus pulled up and the 30-50 waiting soldiers were on their way to basic training. Rourk walked down the aisle and sat in the first outside seat, next to a skinny boy with blond hair, pale skin, and light blue eyes. The kid started rambling immediately. Rourk wished he had picked another seat.

"Hey, so are you also going into the 18X program to try out for Special Forces?"

Rourk looked over at the kid and thought,

You have to be kidding me. "Yes."

"That's awesome. It will be nice to already know someone. My name is Tommy, by the way." He stuck his hand out and Rourk grasped it tightly.

Rourk was surprised to see the kid had a firm grip. That usually told a lot about a person. "Rourk."

"Rourk? That's a pretty cool name. Is it your last name or first?"

"First."

"Are you nervous? I'm so nervous I can barely sit still in this seat."

"No."

"You're not nervous? How is that even possible?"

"I've been training for this my whole life."

"Your whole life? You're a funny guy."

Rourk thought, *Sure, I'm a laugh a minute.* "How long have you been training, Tommy?"

"On and off for about three months. The last 6 weeks I finally took serious. I did a lot of running and push ups."

"Did you run with a weighted rucksack?"

Tommy looked at him like he was crazy. "No, I just ran."

This kid doesn't stand a chance.

"So Rourk, do you have a girlfriend?" Tommy asked, swiftly changing the subject. "I have one and we plan on getting married once I graduate. Here, you want to see a picture?" Tommy scrolled through some pics on his phone and stopped at a pretty girl with brown hair.

"This is Jessica. We've been dating about four months."

"She looks nice."

"What about you, do you have girl back home?"

Rourk thought of Keegan and what a mess that was, then replied. "No." It was no one's business what went on in his personal life. He wasn't about to tell his life story to a stranger.

"That's too bad, Rourk. Maybe you'll meet a girl after we're done training."

"I don't care about girls, Tommy. Right now my sole focus is earning a green beret."

"Sure, that would be nice. You still need a girl, though." Tommy laughed and jovially hit Rourk on the side of his arm.

Tommy rambled on for another twenty minutes. Rourk just nodded when it seemed appropriate.

Finally, Rourk leaned his head against the glass and pretended to be asleep. In the darkness behind his eyelids, he tried to locate Keegan, but it was impossible. He missed seeing her. The longer it went on, the more he felt he would do anything to bring their bond back. He tried not to think about her with the shape shifter; it upset him too much.

Instead, he thought about what lay ahead. He would be spending at least sixteen weeks at Fort Benning, Georgia. Nine weeks of initial infantry training, four weeks of advanced individual training, and three weeks of airborne training. That was just the beginning. He wasn't concerned, although he did feel bad for the kid sitting beside him.

He must have dozed off, because the next thing he knew the bus had stopped and they were being herded off like a bunch of cattle.

The screaming started as soon as they got off the bus.

"Throw your bags in a pile. You guys are pathetic!" one of the drill sergeants yelled.

A few minutes later, a different drill sergeant screamed, "Pick up your shit, and you better not get it messed up!"

It was complete chaos. Rourk stood back and watched as all the recruits ran around like chickens with their heads cut off. One of the drill sergeants yelled at Rourk to grab his stuff, so he just picked up anything and walked over to the line. He had to hide a smile as he watched them all run in circles.

He had done many such tricks with his own soldiers when he was an instructor for the young boys training for the elfin army. There was no way they could get the right gear. It would be sorted out later. He noticed Tommy was looking lost and scared. Rourk walked over to him and handed the kid the gear he was holding then told him to get in line.

"Thanks so much, Rourk. I owe you. This shit is scary man." The poor kid's face was white and his hands were trembling.

Rourk laughed. "Tommy, you haven't seen anything yet."

Rourk grabbed another set of gear and took his place in line next to Tommy. He'd try to look out for him, at least for a little while. Right now, all that was going on were mind games. It would be interesting to see how many of the guys broke before the week was over.

When they went to their assigned rooms,

Rourk could have laughed when he saw that Tommy had the bunk under his. *It's funny the way life throws someone in your path.* That cemented it. He would do everything he could to try to help Tommy make it through this nonsense.

"Hey, Tommy. Looks like were stuck together for a while."

"Rourk, I have never been so happy to see someone in my life," Tommy answered, clapping Rourk on the shoulder. "Thanks again for helping me earlier."

"Listen, Tommy, everything they're going to do for the next few weeks is nothing but mind games. They want to break people so they can sort out the weak from the rest. Every time you are scared or don't think you can make it, remind yourself: It's all mind games. Countless others have made it and so can I. Repeat that to me."

Tommy repeated, "It's all mind games. Countless others have made it and so can I."

"That is your mantra for the next few weeks. I want you to say it to yourself before you go to bed, when you wake up, while you eat, and whenever you doubt yourself during the day. When you're being screamed at, just look straight ahead and repeat your mantra. Do you understand?"

"Umm, sure Rourk. If you think it will help. At this point I'm willing to try anything and we're only at day one. I'm glad you're my buddy."

"Get some sleep. We'll be woken up before the sun."

"Night Rourk, and I meant it man, we are going to find you a girl once we're out of here."

"Goodnight, Tommy."

Rourk didn't bother to get under his blankets

because he knew it would be a waste of time to make up the bed in the morning. He closed his eyes and willed himself to fall asleep.

Inhaling deeply, he swore he could smell a hint of sandalwood and vanilla, Keegan's smell. He needed to pull himself together. Rourk placed his hand behind his head and closed his eyes, thinking about when he would see her again. On her birthday. He wondered if he should give her the present he had planned on or if that would upset her. Maybe he should just find a normal gift instead of giving her something that once belonged to his mother. He could always get her the new lens she wanted. Rourk smiled and pictured her on the rocks in the creek, taking photos.

It helped him drift off to sleep.

Chapter 12

Keegan woke up thinking about Rourk.

It had been six weeks since he had left, and it was still hard for her to believe he was gone. She wondered how he was doing and if he had already started basic training. She had a feeling she would not hear from him again until her birthday. The thought made her sad even though she wasn't sure why.

Her mood lifted when she thought of the date she had with Donald later that evening. He was so funny. They had been spending a lot of time together, and she hadn't had an anger incident since the first time in Calvron's world. It was hard to get angry when Donald was around because he always kept her laughing. He made her feel like the most important person in the world. He was obviously crazy about her and not afraid to show it or let the whole world know.

They were now officially a couple. She had to admit they did look cute together. Though, there was still a nagging feeling in the back of her mind that she wasn't being fair to Rourk.

Tonight, they were going to go ice-skating. Donald thought it was funny when he told her that if she got angry on the ice, no one would realize. She smiled to herself as she tossed her blankets to the side and crawled out of bed. Checking her phone, she found a couple of texts from Lauren and Anna. They were finally going back to the magical land!

Keegan was super excited and ran to tell her brother.

She skidded to a stop at his doorway, not bothering to knock as she threw it open. "Thaddeus, we're going to the magic land I told you about. Do you want to come? You can even bring Sam. Calvron isn't grounded this weekend."

Thad looked up from his Xbox, totally unfazed. "What time are you going?"

"Around noon."

"Sure, I'll go. Can we pick up Sam on the way?"

"Of course. You know I love Sammy."

Keegan had about two hours to waste so she headed downstairs to see what her parents were up to and to play with Warrick. She had forgotten her father was gone, so it was just her mom and Warrick.

Warrick was in his corner playing with blocks, as usual. He was obsessed with those things. When he saw Keegan he jumped and ran squealing into her arms. "Kee-Kee!" She loved that kid.

"Vroom Vroom." She started running in circles with him. Warrick giggled loudly. Finally, she let him down which made him very unhappy, and he screamed at the top of his lungs to show his displeasure. She left him for her mother to deal with.

What to eat? Opening and closing the cabinet doors, Keegan found nothing that looked appealing. "Mom, can you make some french toast and bacon?"

"Keegan, you need to learn to cook. How are you going to survive college next year?" Emerald was at the kitchen table with Warrick in her lap and her laptop open in front of her as she paid bills online.

Keegan shrugged. "Pizza and canned food."

"That's healthy." Her mom stood up with Warrick on her hip and handed him to Keegan before gathering what she needed to make breakfast.

"So, what are you up to today?"

"I'm going to take Thad to that magical land Calvron creates." She tossed her brother in the air, and he had a giggling fit.

"Really? Well, that's nice of you to include your brother." Her mom glanced at her with a smile while she was cracking the eggs.

The bacon was sizzling on the stove. Keegan loved the smell. "Yeah, it should be fun. I wish you could come see it, but I don't think adults are allowed."

"Too bad you couldn't take pictures."

"Yeah, I asked Calvron and he said they would just show up blank." Keegan put Warrick in his high chair and got out his favorite snack, Cheerios, which he immediately started tossing on the ground.

"Magic and modern technologies don't work well together."

"It sucks. How cool would that be to have pictures of that amazing world?"

Emerald dipped the bread slices in the egg mixture as she asked, "Is Calvron still going out with Lauren's sister?"

"Yep, they seem to really be into each other. Calvron probably cast a spell on her or something." Keegan grinned.

After dropping the french toast in the skillet, her mom turned to face her. "How are things with Donald?" Her voice was nonchalant and her face carefully empty of emotion, but Keegan knew her mother didn't approve.

"Fine, we are having tons of fun hanging out. Tonight we're going ice-skating."

"Is it serious?"

"Mom, it hasn't even been that long. Who knows what will happen? Don't worry, I haven't forgotten about Rourk." Keegan could feel the annoyance rising in her.

Her mother must have noticed too because she changed the subject. "I haven't seen Lauren and Anna lately. You should invite them over for a sleep-over. We could have a cookout, make S'mores and learn more about their magical abilities."

"Sure, I'll invite them over soon. We haven't had much girl time lately. I've been spending all my time with Donald, and Lauren has been with Josh."

"Anna is probably feeling left out," her mom said as she finally set the plate of food down in front of Keegan.

"Oh my god, Mom, this is amazing," Keegan groaned, her mouth full of food.

"Keegan, don't talk with your mouth full. It's gross." Emerald rolled her eyes as she placed her cup of tea on the table and sat next to Keegan. The baby was still tossing Cheerios all over the floor. They both pretended not to notice. "How is Anna handling everything with her mom?"

"I don't know. She hasn't really talked about it."

"Maybe I should call and check on Jennifer. I can never repay her for bringing you back to us."

"I'm sure she'd like that." Keegan got up and put her dishes in the sink. "I'm going to jump in the shower and start getting ready."

"Well, have fun. I'm meeting Brigid and Katrina for lunch. I should be home before you get back. If not, make sure to text me when you get home."

"Yeah, yeah." Keegan took the stairs two at a time, excited to go back to the magical land. She really hoped she didn't have any issues with her temper today.

After a swift shower and change of clothes, it was time to leave. The weather was starting to get cold so Keegan grabbed her pea coat before heading out the door with Thaddeus. "We have to pick up Donald on the way to get Sammy."

"He hates when you call him that." Thaddeus sighed, tugging his gray hooded sweatshirt over his head as they opened their car doors.

"I know." Keegan laughed.

Keegan pulled up in front of Donald's house a few moments later, and he came out before she had time to text him to let him know she was there. Her face lit up when she saw the door open. She loved his lazy gait. He looked so cute in his Green Lantern t-shirt that was pulled snugly across his chest. As he approached her side of the Jeep, she rolled down her window. He leaned in and gave her a quick kiss.

"You're looking even more beautiful than usual," he said, grinning. Keegan could feel the blush creep up her face.

"Gross! Just get in the Jeep," Thaddeus said from the backseat.

Donald climbed in, shooting an apologetic look over his shoulder. "Sorry, I didn't know you were back there."

"Whatever, let's go get Sam."

Once they picked up Sam, they headed back to the same spot as before. The big wooden door had been replaced with what appeared to be a mirror just hanging in the air by itself.

"That's pretty cool." Sam said from the backseat. He was a tall, lanky kid with sandy blonde hair and pale green eyes. Keegan wondered if he and Thad had planned their clothes because they were both in plain gray hoodies and blue jeans.

"Come on, let's get out there." Keegan jumped out of the Jeep and rushed for the mirror.

No one else was around. Donald reached forward and touched the glass with his hand, and his fingers when straight through. "Well, this is new. Calvron is always coming up with the oddest things. Let's go through and see what awaits us on the other side." He waggled his fingers in the air, making spooky noises.

Donald went first. Keegan made Thaddeus

and Sam hold her hands so they could all go through at the same time.

Calvron had outdone himself once again. Even Thaddeus was impressed.

It was as if they were walking on clouds and there was a huge ancient city suspended in the air. Golden temples and buildings stretched as far as they could see, the sun brightly shining. Every step they took it felt like they were going to fall through.

"Don't worry, you're safe. Calvron would never let anyone get hurt in his land," Donald reassured Keegan as he noticed her hesitation.

With that Keegan took off in a run, her laugh echoing. Donald morphed swiftly into a tiger and chased after her, the two of them disappearing in the clouds.

Thaddeus and Sam looked at each other, shrugged and headed towards the main building. Thaddeus was hoping to run into Anna. They had to discuss some things, but for now, he might as well enjoy hanging out in this alternate world.

"Hey, look at your clothes." Sam pointed at Thaddeus.

Thaddeus looked down. "Awesome."

They were dressed in ancient gladiator wear.

"Come on, let's go see what is inside!" he told Sam, beating on his armor.

He completely forgot about Anna.

Chapter 13

Anna walked through the door at home, exhausted after being out all day with Keegan and the rest of the crew. All she really wanted to do was grab a sandwich and trudge up to her room.

"Anna, guess what?" Her mother walked in from the kitchen. Anna groaned inwardly. She just wanted to be left alone.

"No idea, Mom." She hung up her jacket and sunk into the couch. She knew she couldn't run up to her room if her mother was in talkative mood.

"I've found Magdalena, and you will not believe the luck. She lives only thirty minutes away." Her eyes sparkled when she was happy. Her laugh lines were well-earned.

"You mean you found the light witch?" Anna clasped her hand over her mouth. She was no longer tired. "Did you talk to her? Does she know about me? Did she agree to see me? I wonder if she'll like me."

"Slow down sweetie. Yes, yes, yes, and yes. She wants to meet you right away, as soon as possible. I told her you could come over tomorrow around ten. I hope that is ok with you?"

"Is that ok with me? Ah, yeah! I've been waiting so long for someone to help me. I really hope she likes me. What am I going to wear? I can't believe I just said that, I sounded like Keegan. Speaking of Keegan, I need to call her." Anna hopped to her feet.

"Not so fast. Remember you can't get her hopes up. Do not say anything to her about trying to get the bond back. You promised me, Anna." Her mother looked at her with pleading eyes.

"I won't say anything. I just want to tell her that I have someone that can help me develop as a witch." She walked away, already on the phone with Keegan. They talked for a few moments. Anna had to pull the phone away when Keegan was squealing with excitement on the other end.

Keegan said, "I'm just happy for you to have someone to help you with your gift. This is so exciting."

After she said goodbye to Keegan, Anna made herself a ham and cheese sandwich with mayo and pickles. Grabbing a bag of chips, she sat on the stool and imagined how awesome the next day was going to be.

Her mind filled with images of meeting her first, real light witch. What would she look like? Would she be able to tell that the woman was a witch? She wanted to tell Xavier about it, but he was a human and unaware of her lineage. *Probably not a good idea.*

When she finally went to her room to try to

get some sleep, she ended up tossing and turning all night. She was too excited to sleep. She must have dozed off because the next thing she knew, her mom was knocking on her door telling her it was nine. She only had thirty minutes to get ready!

Okay, calm down, she told herself. *Just throw on some clothes.* Anna tossed almost all of her clothes on the floor—nothing seemed right.

Just as she was about to scream into her pillow, her mother walked in the door and smiled.

"It's okay, Anna. Breathe." She glanced around the room, zeroing in on a pair of black skinny jeans. Picking them up, she handed them to Anna. "Here, wear this. And..." Perusing her daughter's closet, she found a flowing, green shirt and tossed it to her. "And that."

"Thanks, Mom." Anna gave her a grateful smile, clutching the clothes to her chest.

"Breakfast? You should probably eat something."

"I'm too nervous to eat," Anna replied, yanking the shirt over her tank top.

Narrowing her eyes, her mother said, "I'll get you a granola bar and some OJ."

Anna was so nervous she could hardly sit still on the drive. Her mom had plugged the address into the GPS so she wouldn't get lost, which meant Anna was able to arrive promptly and with minimal effort.

Anna pulled up to the house and put the car in park and stared. *You have to be kidding me.*

There was a mini-van parked in the driveway and a white picket fence, complete with flowers, surrounding a two-story, ranch home. It was not at all what Anna had expected. She thought it would be some cool hidden house off the beaten path, maybe bats in the attic and cobwebs on the front porch.

Not Suzie Homemaker in the suburbs.

One last look in the mirror, and she jumped out, heading for the door with her stomach in knots. She rang the door bell.

A stereotypical soccer mom answered. The woman had short, wavy dull brown hair, and a plain face. Her nose was slightly too large, her lips were thin, and her eyes were too close together. She did have a beautiful smile that somehow smoothed over the flaws. She was even in soccer mom clothes: a matching, pink velour jumpsuit.

"You must be Anna," she said with a lovely smile. "Please, come in." She held the door open to allow Anna to pass through.

Anna knew she was staring at the light witch but she couldn't help it. It was so far from what she'd thought that she couldn't wrap her head around it.

Magdalena laughed as she closed the door behind Anna. "You look surprised. Not quite what you expected?"

"Umm, I'm not sure what I expected, but you're right. I am a little surprised."

"Were you expecting something more along the lines of this?" Magdalena snapped her fingers and was replaced instantly by a beautiful woman with long dark hair, perfectly proportioned face, and a smile that could light up the room. She still looked similar to the woman that opened the door, just a beautiful version. She was wearing a long flowing black robe, with purple and gold cords hanging around her neck.

"Yes, I was expecting you to look exactly like this." Anna's cheeks flushed a deep red.

"It's okay, Anna. I have just toned myself down to blend better with the humans. When I am home and the doors are locked, this is how I look in my true form. Let's go into the den."

Anna followed her into the den, looking around the immaculate house still in awe by what had transpired.

Magdalena's home was pretty normal. Her walls were painted in warm earth tones and her furniture was a mish-mash of well-worn antiques. Beautiful nature paintings adorned the walls, lit by the overabundance of natural light that came through the windows. It was pretty and serene. She still had a flat-screen television in front of the couch and a laptop on a corner desk.

Magdalena gestured for Anna to sit at the large wooden table as they passed through a swinging door into the kitchen. "Would you like something to drink? I have iced tea and sodas."

"Iced tea would be great."

The light witch drifted to the refrigerator on silent feet, pulling out a pitcher of dark tea. She filled a glass and sat it before Anna with a plate of cookies.

"Anna, I would like you to show me what you can do with magic," she finally said as she took a seat across from Anna and looked at her expectantly.

"Um, okay. I really can't do much. I haven't been trained." She opened her palms and smiled as the flames appeared. Surely, that would impress Magdalena.

"What else can you do?"

"That's it." Anna shrugged.

Magdalena's mouth pursed as she studied her. "What do you mean, that is it?"

"That's all I can do." Embarrassed, Anna looked away, taking a sip of her tea. It was some kind of fruity tea, and it was delicious.

"How did you learn to conjure the fire?" Magdalena inquired, sitting forward with her elbows on the table.

"I'm not sure. I saw a witch on TV do it so I figured I'd give it a try. It took about a dozen times till I could finally get it to work."

"What were you thinking when the flames came out?"

"Well, for a while I tried chanting *fire fire come alive*. That didn't work. I tried screaming and jumping around but that didn't work either. Eventually, I gave up and sat on my bed to read. I figured I'd give it one more go, so I closed my eyes, took some deep breaths and relaxed my mind. I visualized the fire and there it was. It was quite amazing, if I do say so myself."

"Anna, you have so much to learn," Magdalena sighed, rubbing her forehead. "I wish I had met you years ago."

"You're not the only one," Anna mumbled under her breath.

The light witch stood abruptly and held up a finger before walking out of the room. Anna drank the rest of her tea while she waited, gazing around the kitchen. What little wall space that wasn't covered by white cabinets was pale purple. A small window over the sink looked out over rolling hills, and a pair of glass double doors opened out into a small backyard.

When Magdalena returned a moment later, she had a satchel in one hand. Pulling out a notebook and pen, she opened both and said, "I'm going to give you some exercises, but first I want to know something. Is there anything in particular you would like to learn or study?"

"Actually, there is," Anna said, rotating her empty glass absently on the table. "I'm not sure if my mom told you that she brought my friend back to life by using black magic?"

"Yes, she mentioned that when we spoke." Magdalena's face was empty of emotion.

"Well, my friend, Keegan, is an elf. I was kinda hoping you could teach me how to get back the bond between her and her chosen. The black magic seems to have broken it."

"I see." Magdalena nodded slowly, making a note in her notebook before looking up at her seriously. "Anna, I am going to tell you right now. I will not help you get your friend's bond back. I will teach you the way of the witch, if you are willing to follow my instructions and really want to learn."

Anna tried to compose herself though the anger filled her. "Why won't you teach me about the bond?"

"Because, that is not the right reason to learn the way of the witch, especially the way of the light witch." Magdalena put her palms flat on the table. "I don't teach or practice dark magic, and any kind of spell dealing with dark magic is far out of your grasp right now, anyway. You will be starting from the beginning. The first thing you need to understand about magic is there are certain rules you must follow. One of those is that you mustn't interfere with others' free will. Sometimes, you just need to let life take its course."

"Fine," Anna answered shortly, peeved at the change in plans but determined to see her training through. She couldn't understand why everyone was making such a big deal about it. Was it really so horrible that she wanted to help her friend? "So I guess you won't tell me how I can win over Xavier? My best friend I've been crushing on forever?"

"Anna, you need to take this serious."

"I was just kidding." Anna sighed. "What do you want me to do first?"

"The most important part of your training," Magdalena told her, gesturing for Anna to follow her to the living room. "Will be keeping a Book of Shadows."

"I get my own Book of Shadows? Like on *Charmed*? Cool!"

"This isn't a game, Anna, or a television show. A Book of Shadows is like a witch's diary." She gestured at a small bookcase near her computer desk. It was full of small journals, some of them with cracked and broken bindings while some looked shiny and new. "In it, you record your thoughts, feelings, poetry, successes and failures in spellwork, and anything else for which you need it. Consider it a journal of your magic."

"Are these all yours?"

Magdalena nodded. "All of them except this corner of the top shelf. These are blank. I want you to pick one that speaks to you."

"To keep?" Anna looked up at her, puzzled.

She laughed. "Yes, to keep. You must start using it right away."

Anna stepped forward, kneeling to run her fingers across the spines of the empty notebooks. She slid a few out to see their covers. "They're so plain."

"The inside is what matters, Anna. You'll find that to hold true across all aspects of life." Magdalena gave her a beautiful smile, the kind that reached and crinkled her eyes. "A simple Book of Shadows isn't ostentatious. A witch should never draw attention to herself."

There was one book, a thick, black leather-bound to which she kept returning. It seemed to hum beneath her fingertips. Pulling it from between the other books, she held it in both her hands and smiled.

"This one. Though, I really expected it to look different."

Magdalena shook her head, amused. "Oh, Anna. You have so far to go. Let's talk about what you need to do first, okay? Bring your journal."

They headed back to the kitchen table, where Magdalena handed her a pen. "I have two things for you to do over the next week, and you have to promise to remember to do them."

Anna nodded, opening her journal and putting the day's date in big block letters at the top of the first page.

"Every day for the next seven days, I want you to experience the sunrise and sunset."

"Um, what?"

"In the morning, you are to get up before sunrise and find a spot outside where you can easily see the sun crest over the horizon. Stay until it has fully risen, marking down in your Book of Shadows every sensation and every thought you have while you observe. Consider all five of your senses and write down every thought, no matter how mundane."

"Oka-ay." Anna drew out the word, confused, but made a note in her journal.

"Then, you will do the same each evening with the sunset. Seven sunrises and seven sunsets. I expect you to have many pages of notes to go over with me when we meet a week from today. You can begin with the sunset tonight."

"That's it?"

"That is it, for now. Believe me, Anna, your journey has only just begun."

Chapter 14

Keegan came down the stairs in her pajamas, still yawning. Her mom was typing away on the computer at the kitchen table, her ever present mug of tea at her elbow. Her mother glanced up, giving her a brief smile. "We're going to Italy next week."

"What? I thought we were going to Sri Lanka." Keegan opened the refrigerator, hanging on the door as she searched for something to drink.

"It's too unstable there right now. We haven't been on a cruise in a while. You know that's your brother's favorite, and it's his turn to choose."

"Well, Italy sounds cool. When are we leaving?"

"Thursday, since you have some time off from school for the holidays."

Keegan suddenly got an idea as she grabbed the orange juice and closed the door. She carefully avoided her mom's eyes as she grabbed a cup from the cabinet and said, "Can Donald come with us?"

"Of course not," Emerald answered sharply. "Have you lost your mind, Keegan?"

"Why not? You let Rourk go away with us to the cabin."

"That was under different circumstances. Besides Rourk is your chosen, not just some boy you're dating. You are not eighteen yet." Her mother went back to typing on her computer, dismissing Keegan.

"You are being so unfair, Mom. He could stay in Thaddeus's room. It's not like we're doing anything."

"I said no, Keegan, don't ask again."

Keegan was getting cold as a familiar anger began coursing through her veins. "He's not just some boy, Mother."

"He's no different from the countless others you have dated."

Keegan glared at her mother. "Donald is important to me. You need to accept it." She crossed her hands over her chest and rubbed her arms, her body becoming increasingly colder.

"He's not going, so just forget you brought it up."

"You are such a hypocrite..." Keegan started, only to stop speaking as she stared, her mouth gaping open. Her mother was frozen to the computer like a huge block of ice. "Mom, Mom! I'm sorry!"

Keegan ran to the stairs and yelled, "Thaddeus, help me!"

Something in her panicked voice must have gotten through to him because he came running down, almost stumbling over his own feet as he slid to a stop next to Keegan and his mother. "Damn it, Keegan. I told you to keep your anger in check. What were you fighting about?"

"She won't let Donald come on vacation with us."

"Imagine that. She doesn't want her teenage daughter to go to another country with her new boyfriend. Shame on her. Such bad parenting skills."

His sarcasm struck her painfully, and she started crying. "Thaddeus, what is wrong with me? I feel like some kind of freak. Our mother is frozen, and I don't know how to get her unfrozen."

Thaddeus stared at his mom for a few moments. "What did you do last time?"

"Donald helped me. He just told me stories about myself to make me feel better."

"Any story I could think of right now would not make you happy." Thaddeus gave her a dirty look. "Call Donald."

Keegan was skeptical, but she picked up the phone and dialed his number. She filled him in on what had taken place, and he laughed.

"Keegan, I'm glad you want me to go with you, however your mother is right. That is asking too much from her."

"You don't want to go?"

"Don't be ridiculous, of course I would love to go. But we're still in high school and taking your boyfriend on vacation with you isn't something most parents would approve of. To be honest, I don't even think my parents would allow me to go." He paused. "How long are you going to be gone for?"

"I don't know. I got angry at her before I found out the details."

"Even if you were only gone a day, I would miss you."

"Aww, you're so sweet."

From his post beside his mother, Thaddeus rolled his eyes.

"Are we still on for tonight? I'm looking forward to beating you on our dance off. I know how you love *Dance Central*."

Keegan burst out laughing as Donald started singing in her ear.

"Of course, we're still on. I was going to have Anna, Lauren, and their boy toys join us." Keegan smiled.

A loud cracking noise filled the room as her mother broke free from the ice.

"Keegan, this has got to stop," she snapped. "You need to stop having little fits for no good reason. I swear, you act like you're three sometimes." She brushed the ice off her. "I'm going to take a hot shower and change."

"Donald, I have to go," Keegan said quickly before she hung up the phone. Her mother stood to walk out of the room and Keegan reached for her, horrified. "Mom, I'm so sorry. I didn't mean to."

Emerald just eyed her silently for a moment, then left.

"Keegan, you never make things easy," Thaddeus said, rolling his eyes as he walked out of the room.

She was disgusted with herself. Falling into a chair at the table, she stared down at her cell phone, her cheeks hot.

A couple of hours later everyone showed up at Keegan's house. Anna brought pizzas, Lauren brought soda, and the guys just brought themselves. The six of them headed down to the basement. It was a large space set up like a game room even though it rarely got used.

"Who wants to go first? Dance battle mode. Oh yea!" Donald did a little Michael Jackson spin and looked at them expectantly. He was obsessed with the new Xbox Kinect game *Dance Central.*

"I vote we eat first," Josh said and everyone agreed.

After everyone had eaten, Donald couldn't be put off any longer.

"Let's see what you got, Donald." Keegan turned on the TV and Xbox.

"Yes! You are so going down, Keegan. We'll start with an easy one, 'Funkytown'."

Within minutes, they were all cracking up. Keegan didn't stand a chance. She could barely dance because she was laughing so hard. What made it even funnier was the fact that Donald was so serious about it. He was good, even though he did look ridiculous. It just made him even cuter in her eyes. Xavier took a video and said he was going to put it on YouTube with no sound.

They were sweating by the end of the song and Donald was still dancing when Anna and Xavier went. Keegan pulled him down on the couch with her. "That was fun."

"I told you." He reached over and gave her a quick kiss.

Keegan and Lauren were loudly singing "Can't get you out of my head" while Anna and Xavier were fumbling around with the steps. The game was no joke.

Josh didn't stand a chance against Lauren. All of her years as a cheerleader meant she could pick up dance moves quickly. They decided Lauren and Donald should have a big dance off with a level five song, "Satisfaction."

Lauren won. Donald was seriously impressed with her skills. He said he'd have to do some more practicing and have a rematch.

Richard came home and Emerald filled him in on what had happened with Keegan earlier.

"I wish there was something we could do to help her." Emerald stood up and got her husband a drink.

"Maybe we should just let the boy go with us. I could threaten him, and I doubt he'd do anything inappropriate."

"Richard, we can't just keep giving in to her."

"Listen to them all downstairs. How long has it been since we've heard her laughing like that? Maybe he is good for her."

"What about Rourk?" Emerald wanted to know.

"Rourk is a big boy, he can take care of himself. And he's the one that decided to leave. Of course, I would much rather Keegan be with Rourk than a shapeshifter. However, the bottom line is, it's Keegan's choice not ours. She's not a little girl anymore. She will be eighteen before we know it. Maybe if we act like we approve of Donald, she'll get over him quicker. You know forbidden fruit is always sweeter."

"You're probably right. I just wish we could figure out how to get her bond back."

Richard reached across and grabbed his wife's hand. "Emerald, we are so lucky to have her alive. I really just want her to be happy and enjoy the chance she has been given."

"You always know the right thing to say. It's one of the reasons I love you so much."

"I love you. So are we in agreement?" He raised his eyebrow.

"I guess so. I hope I don't regret this."

Donald stayed after everyone else left, the two of them sitting close together on the couch in the basement. They were just talking when Keegan's father yelled down for them to come upstairs. He probably didn't trust them to be alone together.

"Okay, Dad, we'll be right up," Keegan called. Glancing over at Donald, she saw that he looked nervous.

"Don't worry it's probably nothing. My mom probably just wants me to clean up something."

When they got upstairs, Keegan saw her father sitting at the table and thought, *Oh, no.*

Nothing good happened when her parents called for her to meet them at the kitchen table.

"So, I heard about your little incident today, Keegan." Richard had his hands clasped on the table top. He was still in his uniform from camp. With the camouflage and his size, not to mention the bushy beard, he looked threatening. Keegan could feel how nervous Donald was beside her.

"I'm sorry. I didn't mean to." Keegan sighed and sat down at the table. Donald stayed standing by himself.

"Have you been doing the breathing exercises I went over with you?" her father asked. "You're not supposed to do them just when you are angry. You can do them throughout the day."

"Not really. I always forget."

"You need to remember. This cannot happen out in public, Keegan. I'm sure you don't want us to pull you out of school because you can't control your temper."

Panic raced through her. It was her senior year—she couldn't imagine not finishing school with all her friends. "I'll work on it, I promise. Please, don't take me out of school."

Her father turned his attention to Donald, who was trying to appear as inconspicuous as possible. Richard eyed him. "Donald, I heard my daughter wants to bring you on our little vacation. Do you think your parents would allow it?"

Donald stared at Richard. It took him a minute to compose himself. "I'm not sure. To be honest, we don't have a lot of money, so I'm not sure they would."

Richard stood up and walked over to Donald, putting his hand on his shoulder. "We would never take a cent from you or any of Keegan's friends. She often brings Lauren or Anna on trips. If your parents will let you, we would like you to join us. I think we need to get to know more about the person that has caught our daughter's attention."

"I'll talk to them tonight and let Keegan know."

"Donald, I don't think I need to say this out loud. We are trusting you not to do anything inappropriate with our daughter. She has not yet left this house."

"Of course not, sir. I hope you don't think

that is why I'm interested in Keegan." Donald's face flushed a deep shade of red.

"You would be a fool not to be interested in Keegan, she's a terrific girl. Call me Richard. I hate being called sir."

Keegan ran over and hugged her dad. "You are the best dad ever!" Her squeals echoed off the walls as she jumped up and down, "We're going to Italy. I can't believe we are going to Italy! When are we leaving? How long are we going to be gone?"

"Thursday night. You'll have to miss a day of school, but I'm sure you'll get over it," her father said sardonically. "We'll be gone ten days, I believe. Seven nights on the cruise and a couple of nights on land. Your brother is very excited. Now that you are bringing Donald, I'll have him invite Sam. This might actually be a good trip. Hopefully, we won't have to hear you and your brother arguing."

"I think we can manage." Keegan bounced around again. "Ack, I can't believe you are letting Donald go! We'll be good, I promise."

"Famous last words." Richard tried to be surly but he was smiling. His daughter's happiness was infectious.

"Donald, you need to go home and ask your parents. Make sure you text me right away. If they need to talk to my parents, just call my phone." Keegan practically pushed him out the door.

"Where's Mom? She's OK with this?" Keegan asked after she'd waved Donald down the driveway.

"She's not thrilled, but I convinced her. You

owe me one."

"Sure, Dad!" Her mind shifted gears. "I wonder if Mom would like to go shopping. I love shopping for new trips."

Keegan ran up and hugged her dad again, and then barreled up the stairs. She had to text Lauren and Anna to let them know. She was so excited that she could hardly stand it.

She jumped online and searched Italy, even though she wasn't even sure what part they were going to. She really should have asked more details but she was just too excited. Cruises were a quick way to add more countries to her list, so she loved taking them. Keegan walked over to the map on her wall and ran her fingers over all the pins that were sticking out. Ever since she was little, her parents had kept a map of all the places they have visited. Soon, she would have a pin on the big boot.

Keegan headed down the hall for her mom's room so they could talk about the trip.

Chapter 15

Seven weeks had passed since Rourk started basic training.

His days were long and somewhat irritating because he often didn't agree with the instructors' methods of teaching. Even more irritating was the fact he had to sit back and act like he was learning all of it for the first time when he could probably teach it better himself.

He had managed, however, to stay out of trouble and go virtually unnoticed, which was his goal. Well, maybe not completely unnoticed. It was hard to stay invisible when he consistently finished first in everything.

On the diagnostic PT test, only four trainees scored a 300, Rourk being one of them. In both unarmed combatives and pugil stick fighting, Rourk was undefeated. On the rifle qualification, Rourk and one other soldier scored a perfect 40 out of 40 hits.

Tommy on the other hand had not been so

lucky. He was always doing stupid things to draw attention to himself, and there was only so much Rourk could do to help him. Truth be told, he would be shocked if Tommy made it past the first nine weeks.

The kid wouldn't shut up about his girlfriend and how wonderful she was, which was starting to irk Rourk. Every time Tommy mentioned his girlfriend, it was a painful reminder to Rourk that Keegan was no longer his.

Rourk's thoughts were constantly centered on Keegan. He was unable to escape the memories of their short time together and constantly wondered how she was doing. Through Anna and Lauren, he tried to check on her a few times but the three girls were never together.

He needed to practice more restraint because he was starting to feel like a stalker.

As he pushed himself from where he rested on his bunk, he vowed that he would not check up on her any longer. His heart sunk at the idea.

Rourk headed to the shower and quickly hosed off before the water turned cold. When he came back to his bunk, Tommy was sitting on his bed crying. *Now what...* "What's wrong, Tommy?"

"My girl broke up with me. In a god damn letter. She said she had met someone else and didn't think she could wait for me." Another sob ripped from him, and Rourk couldn't help but understand his pain. "I wish I knew who the jerk was, I would beat the shit out of him."

"I'm sorry, Tommy," Rourk said, standing awkwardly over him. "I really am. Don't waste your time being angry at the guy. It's probably better this happened sooner than later. Now you can focus on your training."

Tommy looked down, picking at the blanket and unable to meet Rourk's eyes. "Rourk, I could give a shit about this training. I feel like quitting and running back to her. Maybe she'll give me another chance if I don't join the Army."

"Tommy, would you listen to yourself? You want to give up on your dream for a girl who hasn't even waited a few weeks for you. If she cared about you, she would have waited. You need to make a choice. You can quit now and run home with your tail between your legs or you can act like a man and finish what you started."

Tommy wiped his nose with the back of his shirt, gazing pleadingly at Rourk. "I've wanted to be a Green Beret since I was a little boy, but do you really think I can even make it? I keep messing up and getting in trouble."

"If you want to make it you can, Tommy, but you need to decide here and now if this is what you want. You can throw it all away for a girl who cheated on you or you can move forward with your life-long dream. That is your choice to make."

Tommy laid back on the bed and kicked his feet up on the metal bar. "I want to stay. As much as it sucks, you're right. If she hadn't cheated on me now, she would have sooner or later." He became quiet, and his jaw hardened. "I just really love her. I thought we were going to get married. When we graduated, I was going to buy a ring."

"That's good that you want to stay. Now you need to direct your anger towards your training. I know it's easier said than done. Do this for yourself. I can tell you one thing, a Green Beret would not run home crying because his girl left him. You need to change your mentality starting right now. Let this lesson harden you. Use it to your advantage."

"You sure talk funny, Rourk. I don't know what I would do if you hadn't been here. If you see me off crying in the corner, hit me."

Rourk laughed. "I hope I don't have to do that. Now let's get prepared for tomorrow. Sleep on top of your blankets so you don't have to make it in the morning. Go jump in the shower now so you are not fighting in line in the morning. When you get back, we'll make sure you have everything in order."

"Thanks, Rourk."

Rourk watched as Tommy headed off to the shower, his shoulders slumped and his head down. The boy needed a lecture on perception. He should be holding his head high and back straight, no matter what was going on in his heart and mind. Rourk couldn't help but feel bad for him; he knew what it was like to love someone and not have the feelings returned.

They only had two more weeks of basic training. Rourk would be glad when it was over, although he still had a long way to go before it was really over. They had lost a few guys—some to injuries, some for reasons like Tommy's, and even one who had been considering suicide—but most of them had managed to last.

Thinking of the guys who had left to return home to their women, Rourk thought, *it's crazy how much a girl can mess up a guy's plans*. The more he thought of it, he realized even most wars were started because of a woman. Tommy had made the right decision. At least now he had a goal which would help keep his mind off the pain.

Rourk knew that having a goal didn't always help. No matter what he was doing, Keegan was always in the back of his mind. He wondered if the loss of a human love was felt as deeply as the love of a chosen.

Just looking at Tommy, he figured it had to be pretty close.

Chapter 16

Keegan lugged her bags down the stairs, grunting from the effort as she griped, "This is ridiculous, Mom, I really don't see why we can't teleport. We are wasting so many hours when we could be there in seconds."

Emerald glanced up from where she was clipping her luggage tag into place on her plaid suitcase. She raised an eyebrow at Keegan's load. "I told you, Keegan, we shouldn't misuse magic. We are perfectly capable of flying like normal humans. It will be fun."

Richard appeared in the open front door and looked up, frowning at his daughter. "Keegan, what in the world? I told you that you could only bring one bag."

Keegan rolled her eyes, letting her bags *thunk* on the floor as she came off the staircase. "As if I could fit everything I need in one bag, Dad. It's not like we're just going away for the weekend."

He closed his eyes and sighed, rubbing his

beard. "Well, don't ask us for help. You are responsible for your own luggage."

"Whatever. When are we leaving?"

"In about thirty minutes."

"Where is the itinerary, Richard?" Emerald called from the living room. Keegan stepped over to the archway leading from the foyer. Her mother was on her knees, frantically moving papers around on the coffee table.

"It was right on the table a minute ago," Richard replied, pushing past Keegan to go help her look.

"Well, it's not there now!"

They heard giggling and the three of them looked over to find Warrick in the corner, chewing on the itinerary as if it were candy.

"You have got to be kidding me!" Emerald slammed her hand down on the table, making a crystal candle holder rattle.

"Emerald, just print out another, it's not a big deal," Richard soothed.

"Hello?" Donald called, coming through the still open front door with nothing more than a backpack on his shoulder.

"I like you already, Donald," Richard said, walking over to clap a hand to the boy's shoulder. He glared at his daughter as she came back into the foyer, smiling at Donald. "Keegan, take note. This is how you are supposed to travel. And Donald, not matter how much she pouts, do not help her with her bags."

"Yes, sir. I mean, Richard. Sorry that is going to take some getting used to." Donald grinned nervously.

Keegan thought it was cute how Donald

stuttered when he spoke to her dad.

Once the bags were loaded into the Land Rover, they were on the way. It was an hour's drive to Nashville, and Keegan was peeved that Thaddeus sat between her and Donald. Poor Sammy was stuck in the back with the luggage. It passed quickly, and they arrived at the airport two hours early.

After waiting thirty minutes in line to check-in, the service representative said there wasn't a ticket issued for Warrick. Keegan watched her dad's eyes narrow and his lips tighten as he spoke with the representative, sure signs he was pissed. He had to go through the hassle of getting another ticket issued, a process that took almost an hour.

When they finally made it through security and to the departure gate, the agent frowned at the tickets. "Sir, there's a problem. Are you aware that Warrick's ticket has been issued for economy class while the rest of your party is in business?"

"That is ridiculous," Emerald spat. "He's still under two, so he sits on my lap. He doesn't even have his own seat."

"I'm sorry, ma'am," the agent responded, not sounding sorry at all. "It's going to have to be taken care of before you can board."

After too much back and forth, the ticket was fixed, and they were allowed to board right as the airline made the final boarding call.

"I told you we should have teleported," Keegan said gleefully as they were hurrying down the jetway.

"Shut-up, Keegan," three voices chorused, making her giggle.

Sliding his hand into hers, Donald grinned at Keegan as they walked. "I'm really excited about this trip. We don't get to travel a lot."

"What is it you want to see while we're in Italy?" Keegan asked. They paused to greet the flight attendant, an older blonde woman with a pretty smile, and slowly followed the late boarders down the aisle.

"The Colosseum, I've always wanted to see that. Oh! Will it matter that we don't speak Italian? What do you want to see?"

Keegan quickly got caught up in his excitement and they chatted, holding hands, during the entire flight.

During the layover in Paris, they were told that Warrick's stroller was going all the way to Rome. That meant they had to carry all the bags and the baby instead of using his stroller as a cart, and the Charles de Gaulle airport was huge.

Emerald was not happy.

"Is it too much to ask for some competence in customer service?" she snapped, shifting Warrick to her other hip as they searched for the gate for their connecting flight.

Warrick started screaming, unprovoked, and threw his bottle, which hit a nearby man in the head. After profusely apologizing to the man, in a fit of exasperation, Emerald said, "Fine, you win Keegan. We are teleporting back home."

"Yes!" Keegan was so excited. She had never teleported before. Not to mention she was dying carrying all her luggage, but she wasn't about to admit that to her father.

Of course, her mother was just being

sarcastic.

They arrived in Rome much too early to check into the hotel, so they decided to go for a walk. Thankfully, the hotel had a check room for baggage.

At first, Keegan wasn't very impressed. The hotel seemed run down and even the neighborhood was a bit on the dingy side. It was nothing at all like she had imagined. However, the deeper they walked into the city, the more its beauty started to emerge. She quickly forgot about the long flight, her tired feet, and her aching back and allowed the magic of the ancient city to take over.

"Isn't this amazing?" Keegan murmured, squeezing Donald's hand. "Imagine all the artists and masonries that were involved in building this city."

Donald's whispered answer was awed. "I am speechless. I expected it to be pretty since I've seen pictures, but this is magnificent. I feel so small, as if I don't belong here. This is a place fit for the gods."

Thaddeus and Sam were anxious to go to the Colosseum, so they grabbed a taxi instead of making the hour-long walk. Keegan had to admit it was a breathtaking site. She found it incredible that it was still standing and that so much took place beyond its walls. They signed up for a guided tour, but quickly ditched it when they realized the guide was boring. Everyone wanted to explore on their own.

Keegan could tell the guys were in awe, and as she wandered, she had the fleeting thought that Rourk would have enjoyed it, too. *Where did that come from?* she wondered, remembering a flash of Rourk's soft gray eyes and his tousled dark hair.

She shook herself from her counter-productive thoughts, looking around for the others, and noticed Thaddeus. He was standing as still as a statue with his eyes closed and his face slightly tilted up to the sky. Keegan watched him curiously for several minutes as he did nothing but breathe. She wondered if he was having a vision.

Donald's eyes were large, trying to see everything at once. When he drew near her and spoke, his voice was low and hallowed. "I feel like their ghosts are still here."

Thaddeus, with his eyes still closed, smiled and said, "They are. Some of them couldn't let the place go and still wander around. They seem annoyed that tourists have taken over the grounds."

Eventually, he opened his eyes. Keegan asked, "Were you having a vision?"

"More like a flashback. It was insane, I was actually watching a gladiator contest. You think elves are cool? Those guys were ridiculously crazy. I could feel the ground shake from the roars of the crowd. It was a whole different world back then. Humans have gotten soft."

"I envy your gift, my son," Richard said, walking up in time to catch Thaddeus' explanation. "I would do anything to go back in time and witness what took place here. You can feel the electricity running through even now." He took a deep breath and closed his eyes, a smile on his face as he placed his hand on the marble pillar. With his large, imposing form and thick beard, he could have passed for a gladiator.

"Donald, I also sense the spirits that walk amongst us today. I have traveled far and wide yet I have never felt anything as magnificent as the energy that claims these grounds." He put his arms around Donald and Thaddeus. "Remember this day. This is what we strive to live up to. The history of great warriors."

"Well, warriors," Keegan said with a chuckle as she took Donald's hand. "I'm starving so I think it's time for some pizza. We can't visit Italy and not have a slice or two."

Emerald nodded her agreement. "I agree. Warrick is getting fussy and needs to eat. This was definitely worth the trip. I hope we come back here someday. Perhaps when Warrick is old enough to understand." They all looked over at the baby. He was walking around with a twig, striking the ground with it at odd intervals.

"Perhaps, he already understands." Richard smiled down at his youngest son.

The rest of the day went by in a blur. They walked many miles and saw many beautiful monuments, fountains, and statues. By the time they made it back to the hotel, everyone was ready to crash. There was one more day in Rome and then they were headed to Venice, where the cruise ship would depart.

Chapter 17

They took a train to Venice, which Keegan loved. There was something about a train station that she found very romantic as she watched the people bustling around, getting ready to head off on their own adventures. She thought she probably enjoyed train stations even more than coffee shops.

Keegan pulled out her camera and started snapping pictures of the travelers. She always felt a little odd taking photos of people without their permission, but they were in a public place after all.

As they took their seats on the train, Keegan noticed another elf seated near them. She was beautiful, with long curly red hair to her waist. She had the sides pinned back as if she were trying to show off her pointed ears. She looked very elfish, so Keegan thought her bloodline must be strong.

Keegan glanced over at Donald to see if he

had noticed her, but he was deep in conversation with Thaddeus. Keegan made eye contact with the elf and they exchanged knowing smiles.

Thankfully, Warrick slept almost the whole train ride so they didn't have to listen to him screaming at completely random times as he usually did. Keegan spent most of the ride snapping pictures through the window. She wished the windows had been cleaned. They were so dirty it would take forever to clean up the images on photoshop.

After a while, it was hard to keep her eyes open so she laid her head on Donald's shoulder and dozed off. The next thing she knew, Donald was shaking her awake and laughing as she wiped the drool off her face.

"You missed some." He wiped the corner of her mouth with his sleeve.

"I've always wanted to go to Venice!" she told him excitedly. "I have to get a mask to add to my collection." Jumping up a little too quickly, she hit her head on the overhang. "Ouch."

A parade was passing as they left the train station via a small side road. People were dancing and singing, wearing brightly colored robes and dresses. Some were playing instruments, the music carrying over the exclamations of the crowd lining the street to watch, while some held signs and danced. It appeared to be some kind of festival.

Keegan laughed in delight, jumping out into the street to join them as they danced to the lilting music. She shared smiles with several of the parade members, who clapped their hands to encourage her.

"Keegan! Get back here!" Her mother yelled, irritation in her voice.

Pouting, Keegan danced back to the side of the road as she waved goodbye to the parade-goers.

The streets were lined with shops. Tons of people milled around, chatting and gesturing to one another. It was so bright and cheerful with so much going on around her, Keegan didn't know where to look first. She continued to take photos and thought of how easy it was to get good pictures when the scenery was so amazing.

Venice was beautiful, and exciting. The colorful buildings were so close to the edge of the canals, they seemed to shoot out of the water. Tourists clogged the streets, though Keegan didn't think they could be called streets. *More like a cobblestone maze*, she thought more than once as she followed her family.

The city was bisected by canals, so sections of it were connected by bridge. However, they weren't normal bridges; they were made completely of stairs. That meant Warrick and his stroller had to be carried over every one.

Keegan felt bad for anyone in a wheelchair.

"This place is not stroller friendly at all," Emerald remarked as they hefted Warrick over yet another set of stairs.

"If we ever return, it will be without children." Richard laughed.

"I agree," Emerald said, tossing him a smile, "but I'm glad the kids got to see it. Though it would be better if Warrick was older."

They had some time before they could check into the hotel, so they browsed shops and picked out some souvenirs and gifts. Keegan also got a mask for her collection.

Seeing all the masks lining the shop wall gave her a great idea. She sent Lauren a text. *Great idea. Masquerade theme for our prom.*

Lauren replied back. *Genius. How's trip?*

Amazing

Jealous have fun xoxo

Everyone was pretty tired, so they took a water taxi back to the hotel to get some sleep for the cruise in the morning. Keegan couldn't wait. Cruise ships always had the best food and you could eat as much as you wanted.

Their hotel was dirty and smelly, so Keegan was glad they only had to stay one night.

"Donald, can you come to my room and watch a movie?" Keegan wrapped her arms around his waist.

"I don't think so, Keegan." Her father gave her a stern look.

"Come on, Dad. We aren't going to do anything."

"Why don't you just go to the boys' room and watch a movie?" Her mother was clearly trying to keep the peace.

"Thanks a lot, Mom. As if we haven't had enough of Keegan for one day," Thaddeus grumbled under his breath. "Come on, Sam. Let's at least pick out the movie before she ruins that too."

"You'll live, sweetie," their mother said, rolling her eyes.

"Let's order some room service!" Keegan exclaimed, pulling Donald towards Thaddeus's room.

They stayed up till after midnight, snacking and watching movies, before Keegan headed to her own room.

Donald walked her to her door, their hands swinging playfully between them.

As they came to a stop at her door, he whispered, "Good night," and leaned down to kiss her. Her stomach filled with butterflies at the touch of his hands on her waist, and he pulled her close to him. She fell into his kiss, forgetting anything but how it felt.

When he was gone, Keegan closed the door and leaned back against it. *How can this be wrong when it feels so right?*

Racing across the room, she threw herself on to the bed. She had feelings for Donald, it was true, but despite the way she felt, Rourk still remained in her thoughts.

She thought of her chosen at the oddest times. He was probably doing well at basic training and was almost done by now, or at least the first phase. Her father explained the process to her, and it was a long one. He said Rourk would break many of the records while he was there because he was that good of a solider.

If only she knew more about her chosen. She couldn't even remember what he liked to do. *Maybe I should have given him more of a chance*, she thought, staring at the ceiling. *Too late for that.*

Besides, she had Donald.

Grinning at the thought of him, Keegan rolled off the bed and jumped in the shower. After such a long day of traveling, the hot water felt so good on her skin. She stayed in the shower until it turned cold and then went to bed.

The next morning she was awakened by her brother banging on the door and yelling, "You better get up. The breakfast bar closes in fifteen minutes."

That was enough to get her out of bed. "I'll be right out."

She threw on a pair of worn, blue sweatpants and a school t-shirt. Tossing her hair up in a ponytail, she ran down to eat. It was obvious everyone had been awake much longer than she since they were already showered and ready to go. Keegan wolfed down a couple of croissants, some ham and eggs, and coffee in record time. The food wasn't that good, but she couldn't expect the best from a stinky hotel.

The worst part about a cruise was waiting in the line to get on the ship. That took forever. "Come on, Mom, can't we use magic to skip the line?"

"Keegan, you are getting ridiculous. We'll be onboard before you know it."

An hour later, they were finally able to get to their room and settle in. They decided to grab lunch while they waited for the mandatory safety brief. Keegan refused to go. "I'll just stay in my room and disappear when I hear the door for the check."

Her mom was so fed up with her by that time that she agreed. Keegan grinned and went and laid back on her bed. She'd go through her photos while they wasted an hour or so on the drill. Thirty minutes later she heard the doorknob turn and she felt the familiar tingling as she disappeared. She loved her gift. Too bad she wasn't able to use it more often.

When everyone returned, they went and checked out the boat. It was huge; there were sixteen floors for the guests alone. They had a rock climbing wall, miniature golf, skating rink, basketball, and a cool teen room. Plus all the pools and hot tubs. It was too cold for swimming, but Keegan planned on spending a lot of time in the hot tub.

Later that night, Donald and Keegan decided to go check out the teen hangout. They were having a dance party which of course was right up Donald's alley. Keegan loved dancing with him even if it was somewhat embarrassing. She thought it was so cute that he really thought he was a good dancer. Her favorite part was when a slow song would come on and he would pull her close. The rest of the room seemed to disappear.

"I'm so glad you were able to come." She smiled up at him.

"Me too. I feel like the luckiest guy in the world."

"You are." Keegan laughed and tiptoed to kiss him.

The next morning they docked in Koper, Slovenia, a beautiful little coastal town. It was chilly on the water so they bundled up before they headed out. Keegan pulled on the green sherpa hat she had bought in Nepal that she loved so much, and her new tan mid-length wool coat. Her parents just wanted to go walking and explore the town. Thaddeus and Sam wanted to stay on the boat, big surprise there. They said they wanted to have the arcade to themselves. Her brother was a serious nerd at times.

Keegan looked around trying to figure out what they should do. "Donald, lets go on the horse drawn carriage. I've always wanted to do that."

Donald grabbed her hand and they crossed the street to where the woman was standing on the curb, running a brush over one of her horses. "Can we get a ride?"

"Of course, I can take you around the town if you'd like and we can stop at one of the cafés." Her English was pretty good.

Keegan looked up at Donald and smiled. "That sounds amazing!"

They jumped in and the woman handed them a colorful wool blanket to drape over their legs. Donald wrapped his arm around her, pulling her close to his warmth. Keegan rested her head on his shoulder and sighed. "This is the most romantic thing I've ever done. It's like something out of a movie."

Donald turned her face towards him and leaned down to kiss her softly. Keegan felt like she was floating on air. She didn't think she had ever felt so happy.

The town was beautiful and the cafe was nice and warm. They were friendly, even with the language barrier. Keegan really needed to work on her language skills. All she knew was *ciao*, which was hello and goodbye in Italian.

After the café, the woman took them by an old castle. It was pretty, but also a little creepy.

"Would you like to go on a tour of the castle?"

"Not this time, we just want to stay in the carriage as long as we can." Keegan smiled at the woman.

"I understand. Young love is a beautiful thing."

Keegan blushed. *Were they in love?* Keegan wasn't sure she even knew what it felt like to be in love. Donald squeezed her tighter and ran his hand through her hair, staring deep into her eyes.

Maybe they were.

The next day they got off the cruise in Croatia, another coastal town as lovely as the last. This time, they walked around town with the rest of the family. They stopped at a local café and had some pizza. It was really cold out so they didn't stay off the boat too long. Once back on the ship, Keegan and her mother went and spent some time in the spa.

As they walked through the glass double doors and into the warm reception area of the ship's spa, Keegan's mom put an arm around her shoulders and squeezed. "So what do you want to do, the works or just a massage?"

"Let's do the works since tonight is the formal dinner."

"Ok, but your Dad and I aren't going to the dinner. You know Warrick can't sit through something like that. We'll be eating at the buffet. I think you and Donald are on your own. You won't be able to bribe your brother into getting dressed up."

The spa receptionist escorted them to the relaxation area. Keegan loved being pampered. She figured her mother was just humoring her since this wasn't really her thing.

"I have to admit, Donald is a nice boy. I can see why you are interested in him."

Keegan blushed. "Isn't he so cute, Mom?"

"He is pretty cute. He's got the orange hair going for him." Her mother laughed.

After spending three hours in the spa, they went back to their rooms to get ready for dinner. Keegan loved to dress up. She pulled out her dress and held it up in front of her, spinning around.

They already did her hair and makeup at the salon so all she had to do was slip into the dress. It was a full-length, Grecian-style, dark green dress that flowed around her legs. Keegan slipped on her heels and checked herself out in the mirror. Her hair was up with a couple of loose curls and her makeup was pretty dramatic, especially in the eyes.

Keegan made her way to the boys' room to get Donald. When he opened the door, he took a step back and his eyes widened. "Whoa, Keegan, just when I think you can't get any more beautiful you show up looking like this. Wow."

"Thank you." She twirled around and smiled.

"You're so adorable when you blush from a compliment."

"Well, I guess you'll have to keep giving them to me."

"I don't think that will be a problem."

"Ok, let's go. You know they get cranky when we're late. I want us to get our pictures taken together, too."

Their time on the ship passed in a whirlwind of sun, lazy days, and Donald. Keegan couldn't remember a time when she'd been so happy or at peace. When the time came to return home, she wanted to hold on to him and Italy as long as she could.

Chapter 18

As they were getting into their class-A military dress uniforms, Rourk looked over at Tommy.

The kid was seated on his bed, putting on his boots. His face broke into a huge grin. "We made it, man. I wasn't sure I was going to at times, but thanks to you, we made it."

Rourk smiled. "Enjoy the moment, but don't get too excited. There is still a long journey ahead of us. We still have three weeks left here for airborne before we move on to the big leagues. This will seem like a joke once we start the Special Forces selection process."

Tommy went silent a moment as he buttoned his shirt, then cleared his throat. "Rourk, I'm not sure I'm cut out to be a green beret."

"Nonsense," Rourk said sharply. "Don't ever speak like that again around me. Confidence and a positive attitude will take you a long way."

"What if they separate us?"

"That's a possibility, Tommy. However I have

a feeling we're stuck together through this. Life is funny that way."

"I sure hope you're right."

The barracks were filled with activity and excitement was palpable in the air. It brought a smile to Rourk's face. Human or elfin, soldiers were soldiers. Most were anticipating seeing their family members after so much time apart. Tommy's parents were coming and he seemed to be happy about that. Rourk wondered if he would be the only one without anyone. Probably not.

Because of Christmas, they had two weeks off after graduation. Rourk wasn't sure what he was going to do with his time off. He had debated going home to see Keegan, but he wasn't sure he could handle the rejection. He had been planning on hiking the Appalachian Trail, eventually. Maybe he'd start that to pass the time.

When they were all lined up and their uniforms were inspected, the soldiers were sent out to receive their certificate of completion. Rourk stood straight as a rod when they called his name. He was slightly taken aback when they announced he was the Distinguished Honor Graduate. They gave a speech about him being the top of his class and making them proud. Rourk's eyes scanned the crowd and he was surprised to see his father, Richard, and Thaddeus beaming at him.

His heart dropped; was Keegan there? He looked around but didn't see her anywhere. A wave of sadness washed over him, but he put one foot in front of the other and walked off the stage, hoping his emotions did not show. Everyone clapped and some of the guys chanted

"Kavanaugh."

Rourk should have felt proud of the accomplishment, but all he could feel was a deep emptiness throughout his body. He wanted to be anywhere else.

Once Rourk was able, he walked over to see his father. Greg gave him a hug, much to Rourk's surprise. When they pulled apart, Rourk said, "I didn't expect to see you guys here."

"As if we would miss this day. You make me proud." His father's voice was gruff, as if he were trying to hide his emotions. Rourk thought the gray at his dad's temples was a little more prominent against the rest of his dark hair than it had been before he left.

"Thanks, Dad."

Richard stepped forward and extended his hand which Rourk shook firmly. Thaddeus did the same. Rourk noticed how much taller the kid had gotten in the weeks since he'd last seen him. "It was nice of you guys to come. I'm sure you are busy."

"Don't be ridiculous, of course we are here. Wouldn't miss it for the world. We'll be there when you receive your green beret as well."

"That means a lot." Rourk found himself unconsciously glancing around for Keegan.

Richard noticed and said gently, "I'm sorry, Rourk. She isn't here. We did not even tell her we were coming. Emerald thought it was best."

"I understand. How is she?"

Richard and Thaddeus exchanged a glance before the elder man said, "She is fine. Typical Keegan. We recently returned from a trip so she's settling back in at school."

"Rourk, is this your family?" Tommy came up behind Rourk and put his arm around his shoulder, breaking the gloomy moment.

"Yes, these are family friends Richard and Thaddeus, and this is my father, Greg." As Rourk introduced them, Tommy leaned forward to shake their hands jovially. "Guys, this is Tommy. He's been my bunk mate the last nine weeks."

"Rourk, your dad looks like an action figure," Tommy joked, causing them all to laugh. Greg's brilliant blue eyes sparkled merrily. Turning back to Rourk, Tommy pointed his thumb over his shoulder. "I want you to meet my parents, if that's ok?"

"Of course, Tommy. I'll be right back," Rourk told his father before striding off with his friend.

Richard nudged Greg with his elbow as the two boys walked away, Tommy's hand clasped to Rourk's shoulder companionably. "It's unusual for Rourk to make friends. Let alone with a human."

"I was thinking the same thing."

Thaddeus shifted on his feet. "I had a vision when Tommy approached us. If he had not met Rourk, his life would have ended shortly. Rourk changed his fate."

"Well, then I guess it's a good thing Rourk finally made a friend." Greg stared off at his son who was being introduced to a harmless-looking human family.

There was a cookout of sorts for the newly graduated soldiers, but Rourk just wanted to leave. When he returned from meeting Tommy's family, he grabbed his bag and they headed to the hotel. They were staying at a Crown Plaza so the room was clean and smelled good. It felt like paradise compared to the barracks.

"I'm going to get a shower before we go out to eat," he told his father. Greg just nodded, waving to him absently as he entered his own room.

Rourk tossed his bag on the chair and walked into the bathroom. He leaned his head against the wall of the shower and let the hot water ease his muscles. If only it was that easy to ease the pain in his chest. He closed his eyes and tried to picture Keegan's face and, of course, all he saw was darkness. At least he could take some comfort in the fact that she wasn't given the option of coming. He would hate to know she turned down the chance to see him.

It was hard to believe Christmas was right around the corner. Everyone was excited to have the time off. Rourk just saw it as a delay. He wanted it all to be over with.

As he rinsed off under the stream of water, he realized he hadn't gotten Keegan a gift for Christmas yet. Maybe the other men wouldn't mind stopping at a mall so he could send something home with Richard.

He had already decided he wasn't going to go home.

Rourk was relieved to be out of the uniform and in civilian clothes again. He grabbed his coat and winter cap, and then headed to his father's room, where he called Richard to meet them in the lobby. The food at the military base left a lot to be desired. Rourk wanted steak and potatoes, so they went to a local steakhouse.

"So Rourk, are you coming back home during your break?" Richard asked later as they ate, looking at him over his glass of soda.

"No, I'm going to stay here. I've been thinking of hiking the Appalachian Trail. I'll just start in Georgia, and head north for the two weeks. Once it's time to come back, I'll grab a flight back from wherever I end up, which should be near Virginia. I need some time to think. As you well know, it's easier to think in the woods."

"Would you like company Rourk? I am due for some time off," his father said.

This startled Rourk. His father never wanted to spend time with him anymore. He'd rather be alone, but he couldn't turn down his father. "I would like your company, Father."

"We'll have to make a trip to an outdoors store. I didn't bring the correct gear."

"I wanted to stop and get Keegan a present anyway."

"I wish we could join you but I don't think my mom would be too happy if we missed Christmas." Thaddeus laughed.

After they ate, they went to a mall and Rourk found a camera shop. He knew Keegan had a Nikon, but that was all he knew. He asked what lens was the best, and the clerk showed him three different ones. He got them all. He had nothing else to spend his money on.

The mall didn't have a decent outdoor store so they headed to the nearest REI. His dad bought the gear that was required to go hiking in cold weather. Rourk was starting to look forward to spending time with his father. It had been a long time since they had done anything together. When Rourk was a young boy, they had gone on many long hiking trips together.

The next morning Richard and Thaddeus left for home. They took the easy way and used magic. Rourk had given them Keegan's presents to put under the tree, signing the box Rourk and leaving it at that. He didn't know what to say to her.

Rourk was impatient to go. After they had seen their companions off, he turned to his father. "Want to head out, Dad?"

"Sure, might as well get an early start. Let's grab some breakfast, and then we will get our gear and go." His father smiled warmly.

Rourk took out his GPS and found the nearest opening to the trail as they were walking down to the hotel buffet. "We shouldn't have to worry about seeing too many people at this time of the year."

"I'm sure there were will be a few hard-core hikers out."

Sure enough, they did pass a few guys along the way.

At one point as they were trudging up a hill through ankle-deep snow, Rourk said, "I'm glad you decided to come with me, Dad."

Greg nodded, his hiking stick striking the ground as the crunching of their footsteps filled the silence. "Me too. It's been too long. I know I have been distant since your mother passed away. After the battle in Ireland, I did some deep thinking. I have missed out on so much since your mother died. I need to get back into the real world. I know I will be with her again when it is my time."

Rourk looked over at his father, surprised that he was being so open. "I'm glad to hear that,

Dad."

They continued hiking in silence.

After a while, Rourk broke the silence once more. "Have you seen Keegan?"

"No, son, I'm sorry but I have not. I don't really get out other than going to work."

"Do you think I should give her mom's ring for her birthday like all chosen do?"

Greg seemed lost in his thoughts for several minutes as he tried to form an answer. Rourk waited patiently, watching his breath fog in the cold air until his dad finally answered. "I'm not sure that is a good idea. Maybe you should talk to her first and see what her thoughts are on the whole matter. It might be too much for her to handle, and you don't want to push her away."

"That's what I was thinking. I just wish this had never happened." Rourk kicked the ground with his boot.

"Don't give up. Hopefully, it sorts itself out."

"I hope so. Although, it's not looking too good at the moment."

His father put his arm around his shoulder. "I wish there was something I could do."

They hiked the full two weeks together. The weather was freezing, but neither seemed to notice. They mostly hiked in silence, but when they did talk it was never idle chit chat. Their words always had meaning.

When it was time to say goodbye, Rourk was sad to see his father go, but he was happy to have spent so much time with him. He really hoped that his father had meant it when he said he was going to try to enjoy life more.

Chapter 19

Her grandmother must have been over, because Keegan woke up to the smell of gingerbread.

Jumping out of bed, she was filled with excitement that it was Christmas. *Who doesn't love presents?* she thought with a smile.

She found it hard to believe time had passed so quickly. Keegan looked down and grinned, wiggling her toes in her footed polar bear pajamas. Ever since she was a little girl, her mother had given them Christmas pj's to wear to bed every year on Christmas Eve.

She stretched, went to the bathroom, and then headed downstairs. Halfway down, she realized she had forgotten her camera, so she ran back up to grab it. Once downstairs, she skidded across the wooden floor laughing.

Her father always went out to the woods, and picked the biggest, fattest tree he could find. He outdid himself this year—it was almost touching the ceiling. They had spent a full day decorating it.

Even though they lived out in the middle of the woods, and no one could see them, he also went crazy with lights for the outside of the house. Her father always went over the top for Christmas.

Thaddeus was lounging on the couch in his hooded sweatshirt and new pj pants. He had been given black flannel pants covered in reindeer with strings of lights around their antlers. "Waiting on you as usual, Keegan."

"Well, I'm here now. Let's open some presents. I see Warrick already got started." He was playing with a box and had the wrapping paper covering his head. He was a little clown. She snapped a picture.

"Hey Nanny, I can't wait till you see the present I got you."

Her grandmother walked over and kissed the top of her head. "I'm sure I'll love it."

"Ok, dig in everyone." Her father tossed a present to Keegan.

She got the usual: tons of clothes and gift cards. Her father got her a cool tripod she could use in the woods. It would attach to almost anything.

One section under the Christmas tree was dedicated to their household, and there was one box left. There were still piles of presents for the rest of the extended family.

"Whose is this?" Keegan asked as she picked up the present and shook it. The room was oddly quiet. She looked at the card.

It said *To Keegan, From Rourk.*

Keegan sat down on the floor and crossed her legs, staring at the box in front of her. She felt bad that she didn't get him anything.

Slowly, she opened the box and started squealing at the three lenses. "I've wanted a new lens forever."

"That was really sweet of him," her mother said from across the room.

"I know, I feel bad I didn't get him anything," Keegan answered as she attached one of the new lenses to her camera.

"Well, maybe you can send him some photos you took. I know when I was in training, I loved getting mail." Her father smiled at the memory.

"That's a great idea. Let me get a picture of all of you near the tree."

A couple of hours later, Donald showed up for dinner. He had become a regular at their house. He gave her mother a new teapot, which she loved, and gave her father a book for his library. Thaddeus got a gift card with Xbox points.

"I'm sorry. I didn't know you were going to be here," Donald told Keegan's grandmother. He was obviously embarrassed.

"Don't be ridiculous. I'm old and have everything I want. Just come over here and give me a hug."

After hugging Mary, Donald pulled a small box out of his coat. "I got this for you, Keegan. I wish I could have gotten you more. But, there's only so much snow shoveling to be done in Tennessee to make extra money," he said, making everybody laugh.

Keegan smiled and slowly unwrapped the present. It was a pair of silver dolphin earrings with a small blue stones for eyes. "I love them! Thank you." She put them in her ears right away with a big grin.

"I know how you love dolphins. I'm glad you liked them. I wasn't quite sure what to get you."

"Can you take a picture of me with them on?" Keegan handed Donald her camera.

"Nice, I see you got a new lens for Christmas." He snapped a picture.

"Yes, I actually got three."

"I know you will have fun with that. Santa was good to you this year."

Keegan looked down, biting her lip. "Rourk sent them."

"Oh." Everyone was quiet.

Warrick squealed out to break the awkwardness.

"That was nice of him," Donald said as he handed the camera back to Keegan.

She could tell he was uncomfortable.

"Keegan, why don't you take Donald into the den while we finish cooking in here?" Her mother practically pushed them out of the kitchen.

Keegan put her arm around his waist as they walked into the den. "You don't have anything to worry about with Rourk."

"Are you sure, Keegan? He is your chosen, after all."

"My bond to him has not returned, and I don't think there is any possibility it will. He is a stranger to me. It's you I care about."

Donald paused just inside the door of the living room, turning to face her. His eyes searched her face as he brushed her hair back with one hand. He took a deep breath. "I love you, Keegan. I know I haven't said it before, but it's true. I've loved you for as long as I can remember. I'm terrified I am going to lose you to him."

Keegan didn't know what to say. She wrapped her arms around herself, staring wide-eyed at him. Why weren't the words rolling off her tongue as easy as they did his? "I really love the earrings you got me."

"Smooth change of the subject." Donald quirked an eyebrow at her, pulling on her elbows until she put her hands in his. "I understand if you can't say the words yet. I hope in time you will be able to look me in the eyes and tell me you love me."

Keegan thought about her words before she spoke. "I do care about you. I have been so happy during our time together. I love the way you make me feel."

They sat together on the couch in front of the tree. Keegan liked the way the colorful lights blinked on and off on his hair.

"I guess I will have to settle with that for now." Donald pressed a light kiss to her temple before saying quietly, "I applied for a couple of colleges in Alaska."

"You did?" Why did she feel so strange about this revelation?

"I just can't stand the thought of being so far apart from you. I really don't care where I go to school. I've never had a favorite college that I wanted to attend to. They have plenty of good engineer programs in Alaska."

"I hope you applied to other schools, as well, so you have a choice?"

"Yes, I applied to several. A couple in Tennessee, Florida, and California."

Keegan felt slightly relieved to hear this. She had already received her early acceptance to the college of her choice in Alaska. Her mother was going to take her to check it out soon.

"I think our conversation is much too serious to have on Christmas day. You haven't even opened your present from me." Keegan ran up to her room and came down with a box.

She watched as he tore open the present and a smile spread across his face. "Keegan, this is too much. I can't accept this."

"Shhh, how else are you going to beat Lauren unless you are able to practice?"

"Thank you." He leaned over and kissed her deeply as if it were their last kiss.

She had gotten him the Kinect for his Xbox along with the *Dance Dance Revolution* game. Keegan loved giving presents almost as much as she enjoyed receiving them.

"Guys, come on out. It's almost time to eat."

"Well, be right there, Mom."

They walked into the kitchen and saw the rest of the family had arrived while they were chatting in the living room. Keegan's aunts Katrina and Brigid stood at the counter with her mother while all of her cousins milled about, stealing food.

"Hey guys, come get your presents!" Keegan said excitedly, leading the rush to the tree. She started tossing presents at them, laughing as they all tore into them.

Donald put his arm around Keegan. "You seriously have the best family."

"Yea, they aren't so bad." She looked down to find Mackenna wrapped around her leg. Keegan laughed, pinching the little girl's cheek. "Go get your presents, Mack attack."

Mackenna ran off giggling.

The house smelled wonderful. Her grandmother always came over and cooked the holiday meals, so they had a huge turkey, ham, and a roast. Keegan always ate more food than she could handle and ended up uncomfortable for the rest of the night, but it was delicious, anyway.

Chapter 20

Keegan heard a knock at the door. She closed her eyes to see who it was even though she was expecting Anna and Lauren. It was them, and they looked like they were freezing. She ran down the stairs to let them in.

"Mom, can you make us some hot chocolate?" Keegan yelled into the kitchen.

"Of course." Her mom peeked around the corner. "Hi girls, it's nice to see you."

"Hello, Keegan's mom," they said in unison, stomping snow off their boots on the rug outside the door. Frigid air drifted through the door around them, so Keegan quickly ushered them inside.

"Just throw your bags on the floor," Emerald told the girls, disappearing back to the kitchen, presumably to make hot chocolate.

"It's been so long since we've had a sleep over." Keegan hugged them both and then brushed the snow off Anna's shoulder as they pulled off their snow boots.

"I can't wait for the party tonight," Lauren gushed, nearly tripping as she finally yanked her second boot off a little too roughly.

Anna rolled her eyes. "Yay, we get to go to a party at one of your lame cheerleader friends' houses."

"It's not just any house. It's more like a mansion. You will have fun, I promise."

"Don't forget Xavier is going to be there," Keegan teased her.

"I've given up on him. You would know that if you bothered to call me." Anna shot her a bored look.

"Sorry, I know I've been spending more time with Donald and less with you guys." Keegan pouted.

Anna rolled her eyes, hanging her scarf and jacket up in the hall closet. "I haven't even been able to tell you about Magdalena, the light witch that has been helping me with my powers."

"How has that been going?"

Suddenly, Lauren's hat flew off her head and hit Keegan in the face. "Well, I can do that now." Anna laughed.

"Good one." Keegan threw the hat back at her.

"We have so much catching up to do. Let's promise to spend more time together. Before we know it we will all be heading off to different colleges," Lauren said.

That sobered the moment.

Emerald came in with a tray full of hot chocolate and warm cookies. "Come and sit down in the den in front of the fireplace, girls."

They didn't have to be asked twice. They

knelt around the coffee table, helping themselves to the goodies. "This is the best hot chocolate ever," Anna groaned, closing her eyes in ecstasy.

"It's Godiva from the can." Emerald shrugged and smiled.

Thaddeus came barreling down the stairs. "I have to talk to Anna about something."

The girls all looked at each other in surprise. Thaddeus rarely bothered with any of them.

"Um, ok." Anna stood up and followed Thad to the back of the house.

"Keegan told me you were a witch."

"More like a witch in training. Why what's up? You're like all powerful? What do you want with me?" She placed her hand on her hip and stared at him.

"Once again, I am going to break the rules for Keegan. Don't ask me why. She's such a pain. I do like Rourk though, and I want him to be happy."

Anna was getting excited. "I like where this is going. What do you need from me? I have been trying to find a way to get their bond back, but I am having no luck at all."

"Well, I had a vision and the answer came to me. It's so simple, it's almost laughable."

"What is it?" Anna's eyes were wide with excitement.

"It's the ring. The ring is the key to all of this. You know how elves get engaged as soon as the youngest turns eighteen? The ring is what cements the bond."

"Oh my Goddess, are you serious, Thaddeus?" Anna couldn't control her excitement. "Where do I come into all of this?"

"Well, I need you to implant dreams into Rourk's head that make him want to give Keegan the ring. It's the natural thing for him to do, but with the bond broken he might need a nudge in the right direction."

Anna's face fell. "I have no idea how to implant dreams."

"That's okay, I have access to a Book of Shadows. We can figure it out."

"You have a Book of Shadows? Thaddeus, can I kiss you?" She grabbed him by the shoulders and jumped up and down, her brown and purple hair bouncing.

"Gross, no." He gave her a horrified look.

"Okay, but what if Keegan doesn't want to take the ring?"

"That's also where I need your help. I could ask an elfin witch, but they know it's breaking the rules. You never follow the rules so I figured you would be the perfect witch. Not to mention I saw you holding the ring in my vision."

"That's so cool that I was in your vision," Anna gasped, grabbing his arm. "What was I wearing?"

Thaddeus shook her off, rolling his eyes. "Now you're being stupid. Just pay attention. We don't have much time before they wonder what we are up to. You are going to need to spell the ring. Some sort of enchantment spell so it will be impossible for Keegan not to want to try on the ring. Once the ring is on her finger, BAM. The bond is back and sealed."

"Is it really that simple? I have spent months trying to figure this out."

"Magic is often simple." Thaddeus grinned at

her. "Of course you have to keep this to yourself or it won't work. This has to come as a total surprise to both Keegan and Rourk."

"It's going to be hard, but I will keep the secret. I feel like screaming it from the top of a mountain."

"It has to happen on Keegan's birthday," Thaddeus mused, leaning against the wall. "So hopefully the stars align and we can get Rourk back here in time."

"Well, we have a few months so I'm sure it can be worked out. Maybe you can contact his father. The dreams may be enough to pull him back."

Thaddeus nodded. "His father is a last resort. Rourk did tell Keegan he would be back for her on her eighteenth birthday. He is a man of his word. So I'm sure he will be, as long as his training does not interfere."

"When are we going to get to see the Book of Shadows?"

Anna's swift changes of subject were wearying. Thaddeus sighed. "I cannot remove it from the vault so I will have to take you there. It is forbidden for any non elves to enter. We will have to cloak you."

"This is the most excitement I've had in my life," Anna squealed, bouncing up and down again as she clapped. Thaddeus tried to shush her, but it didn't work. "I'm going to a secret vault, I'll be cloaked, and I get to read a Book of Shadows. Are you sure I can't kiss you?"

As she stepped towards him, he bounded quickly away. "Don't even think about it. Get back in the living room and tell them I needed your help on a computer program. They will buy that since you are a computer geek."

"I'm not a computer geek," she argued, but there wasn't a lot of strength behind it.

Thaddeus ignored her. "We'll get together next week and start working on the plan. Wait, what's your cell number? I've been waiting almost a month for you to come by."

"I feel so diabolical," she giggled, sending him a quick text so he would have her number. She gave a wicked laugh, patting him on the head before she headed back to the living room.

She walked casually into the room, hoping her face didn't give away the glee she felt inside.

"What the heck did Thad want you for?" Keegan asked, slurping her hot chocolate.

"He needed some computer help, and he knows I have mad skills. Of course I took care of the problem." Anna gave a low bow, and Lauren clapped.

"Well, we have more important things to talk about. What did you bring to wear for the party?" Lauren raised an eyebrow.

"I brought a short, one-shoulder black dress and sparkly heels. Don't even bother to ask, Keegan. I'm not wearing flats." Anna stuck her tongue out at her friend.

Keegan shook her head and giggled before answering. "Oh, I can't wait to see it on you. What about your hair?"

"Whatever our stylist, Lauren, wants to do with it."

Lauren looked over at Keegan "What about you? It feels odd that we didn't go shopping together."

"You'll have to wait and see."

A few hours later, they were getting ready for the party. Lauren came out of the bathroom wearing a beautiful, strapless purple and black dress. It was short and the bottom flared out with a tulle skirt.

"You are so hot it makes me sick." Keegan grinned to take the sting out of the statement.

"Ok, now go put on your dress. I'm dying to see what you picked out." Lauren pushed her towards the closet.

A few moments later Keegan waked out and did a spin. "What do you think?"

"Keegan! Where did you find that dress?"

"Modcloth.com. They have all kinds of cute, vintage-looking dresses."

"I love that color on you. It's almost the same color as your eyes."

Keegan stared at herself in the mirror, taking in the strapless sweetheart neckline, and she pulled up the rows of gathered silk. She smiled as she touched the bow that completed the dress. "It is pretty cute!"

"You are going to give poor Donald a heart attack."

"Your turn, Anna. Hurry up, we don't have much time."

Anna came out a few moments later, throwing her hands up in the air as she said "Ta da!"

"Wow, all I see is legs and sparkles. Speaking of giving people a heart attack. If Xavier doesn't notice you tonight, he must be blind." Lauren reached out and ran her hands over Anna's sparkles.

"You haven't said much about Josh lately." Keegan looked at her curiously

"We're fine. I'm just thinking that I need to break up with him before I head off to college. He wants to stay in Tennessee, and I don't see that for myself."

"Well, that's too bad. At least you guys have had a couple of good years together," Anna remarked.

"Katrina should be here soon to pick us up. I asked her to drive in case we have a couple of drinks."

"Good thinking. I miss Kat. We haven't seen her in a while."

They ran downstairs when they heard Katrina yell, "Hello, is anyone home?"

"You are such a dork, Katrina, that's why we love you," Keegan greeted her aunt.

Kat looked young and hip in her tight blue jeans and fitted red sweater. She let out a long whistle. "You guys look HOT!"

The girls giggled while bundling up before they made the cold journey to the car.

Lauren wasn't kidding when she said the party was at a mansion. There was an indoor pool and guys were already jumping in it. Keegan noticed Donald over by the pool table. He looked up at the same time, a wide grin spreading across his face as he handed his pool stick to another guy and walked away from the game.

"You are gorgeous," he murmured, one arm curling around her to drag her body against his. "I can't believe you even give me the time of day."

"You are ridiculous. I'm the lucky one." Keegan put her arms around his waist as he leaned down to kiss her.

"Get a room!" someone yelled.

Donald laughed, and Keegan's face turned bright red.

"Let's go dance." Donald pulled her into the next room.

Keegan glanced around and couldn't get over the extravagance of the place. A huge chandler hung above them and tables lined the walls overflowing with food. A live band was playing, complete with light show and disco ball. Keegan barely knew the girl who was throwing the party, but she had gone all out.

She smirked at Donald, amused. "I see you learned some new moves."

"Yep, thanks to your Christmas present. Give me another week and I'm asking Lauren for a rematch."

Keegan glanced around trying to catch a glimpse of Anna or Lauren but there were too many people. "Where are the rest of the guys?"

"No idea, and I don't really care. I just want to be with you." He touched the side of her face and smiled down at her.

"Let's grab a drink before I get dehydrated from all this dancing." Keegan led him off the dance floor and to the food, where she grabbed a plate and filled it with snacks.

"Do you want soda or a drink?" Donald asked.

"Soda or punch is fine."

"Ok, I'll go get in line."

She watched as he walked off with his lazy gait and smiled to herself.

"There you are. I have been looking all over for you!" Lauren screamed over the music.

Keegan raised an eyebrow. "I can hear you fine. What's up and where is Josh?"

"I just broke up with him. He's so upset."

"I thought you were going to wait till the end of the school year?"

"I figured I might as well get it over with now. It's kind of cruel to lead him on."

"That's true. Are you ok?"

"Not really. I need a drink."

"Go tell Donald, he's in the line."

Lauren gave her a thumbs-up and glided away, scanning the drinks line for Donald.

Later, Keegan reflected that telling Lauren to get a drink was probably not the best idea she had ever had. She stood in the bathroom, the sounds of the party muffled by the closed door, and held Lauren's mass of dark curls back as her friend got sick in the toilet.

Supporting a very heavy Lauren on the side of her own body, Keegan escorted her out of the house. The cold air seemed to sober Lauren enough for Keegan to let her fall to the white wicker couch on the front porch while she texted Donald and Anna that they needed to leave.

"Too much?" Donald asked, tugging his big black coat on as he closed the front door behind him.

Keegan turned around to find Lauren had fallen over, her face planted in the cushions as she snored.

"At least she's breathing," Keegan sighed. "Can you take us home?"

"Of course."

Once Anna joined them, they all piled into

Donald's mother's car. Keegan was exhausted by the time she got home and put Lauren in bed.

Chapter 21

Tommy and Rourk both made it through Airborne school.

Rourk was surprised; he ended up having a lot of fun. Tommy struggled because he had a fear of heights. Somehow, with Rourk's encouragement, he managed to make it through unharmed.

Once again, Rourk found himself singled out as the Distinguished Honor Graduate. This time, however, neither Tommy nor Rourk had any family in the crowd.

They were given a weekend pass, before they had to head to Fort Bragg, North Carolina for the Special Forces selection process. The initial selection process was only three weeks long. If they made it through that, it would depend on which field they were placed in. The training would be anywhere from six months to over a year.

Tommy was really nervous that he wouldn't be selected. If Rourk had anything to say about it, he would make it through with flying colors. Having Tommy around made the days go by quicker. Keeping an eye on the kid gave Rourk something to do to keep his mind busy, to keep his thoughts off Keegan. He couldn't help but think that Keegan would really like Tommy. He hoped someday they would be able to meet.

"Come on, Tommy, let's get out of this place," Rourk said, grabbing the last of his things.

Tommy followed suit, checking around the room one last time before he closed the door. "Right behind you. If I never came back to Fort Benning it would be too soon."

"Let's get a hotel downtown. We can get some real food, and maybe catch a movie."

"We should try to get into a bar." Tommy laughed.

"I don't drink, Tommy."

"I'm not talking getting drunk, man. Maybe we could just get a couple of beers."

"My mother was killed by a drunk driver."

Tommy looked stricken. "Oh man, I'm sorry, I had no idea. You're not exactly an open book when it comes to your personal life."

"It's okay. It was a long time ago."

"Maybe we can find a mall and try to pick up some girls."

Rourk stared at Tommy for a moment. Rourk was not interested in girls, but it might do Tommy good to get his mind off his ex-girlfriend. "Sure, we could try that. I'm not very good around females though. So I'll sit back and take notes from you."

Tommy chuckled. "I'll give you some pointers. First one, you need to learn to relax."

Rourk and Tommy caught a taxi to a nearby hotel where they booked separate rooms. They had been bunk mates for so long; some solitude was just what Rourk needed. After they cleaned up, they went out for dinner, then grabbed a taxi to the mall.

It was small and run down. It was already getting dark outside, and shoppers were few and far between.

"I don't know if you are going to have any luck with girls in here, Tommy," Rourk remarked as they strolled down the aisle towards the main shopping area.

"Let's go to the bookstore. There are always hot chicks hanging out there."

Rourk thought of how many times he had seen Keegan getting her white chocolate mocha at bookstores. "Sure, sounds good. I could use a cup of coffee."

They spent a couple of hours at the mall, and Rourk stood back and watched as Tommy got turned down again and again. It was pretty funny, he had to admit.

"One more time, Rourk. Let's go talk to those two girls." He nodded towards a brunette and blond sitting in the food court. Rourk shook his head and followed.

Tommy walked up and put his hand on the table. "So ladies, how would you like to hang out with me and my buddy over there? We're going to be green berets."

The blond looked up at him and said, "Get lost."

Tommy turned towards Rourk and shrugged his shoulders. "Alright, let's go watch a movie."

Rourk had to give him credit for trying—most guys would have given up sooner. A few good movies had come out since they had entered basic training over three months ago, and the thought of relaxing in front of one was a nice one.

It was hard to believe it was already February. Just a few more months until Keegan's birthday.

Once the weekend was over, they were back in their bunks to pack for Ft. Bragg. They were traveling by a van since there weren't many of them left.

"Rourk, I'm scared."

"You should be scared, Tommy. This is the make or break point. If you make it through the next three weeks, more than likely in less than a year you will be wearing a green beret. If you don't make it, you'll be thrown back to the regular army."

"Thanks, that was encouraging."

"Well, you need to know how important this is. I know you can make it."

"You really think I'll make it?"

Rourk smiled over at Tommy. "I really do."

"Well, I can't let you down so I guess I'm going to have to get selected."

"I guess so." Rourk leaned back against the seat and closed his eyes.

"Well, at least we shouldn't have to clean floors once we get there."

"Let's hope not. I've cleaned enough floors and bathrooms to last me a lifetime."

"They didn't tell us that part at the recruiter's." Tommy laughed.

"Yeah, the recruiter seemed to leave out all

the good parts."

Like all training, time seemed to fly. After a couple of weeks of "indoctrination" phase, where they did tons of physical exercise in preparation for the selection phase, they finally got a class date.

They shipped out to Camp MacKall, North Carolina, less than an hour away from Ft. Bragg. The selection class started with 345 "candidates" as they were called. Within the first week, they had lost 50 from the PT test, swim test, and those that chose to leave because they realized they had bitten off more than they could chew.

Rourk and Tommy were in different huts, which was what they called the large barracks buildings the candidates stayed in, but they saw each other several times throughout the day and spent any free time they had hanging out.

The second week was spent running through the woods doing land navigation from point to point. Rourk thought the course lanes were almost laughable in how short they were compared to what he was used to. Each night he checked on Tommy to see how he was doing and to make sure to keep his morale up.

"I don't know man. I only found two points today. I think there were four. They're gonna drop me for sure."

"Relax, Tommy. They don't expect you to do everything perfect. They don't even expect you to find all the points. If you do, it's a bonus. They just want to see that you have the ability to continue to drive on even when things suck. As long as you don't quit and show them you have the drive, you'll make it. You're doing good."

"Easy for you to say. You don't even look tired. I'm beat down. How many points did you find today?"

"Four. After four points, they had me sit over and start up a fire. And I may not seem like it, but I'm tired too. I just happen to be in a little better shape than you. Don't worry about it. Don't think about the negative, just keep thinking about the positive and your mantra. Say it for me."

"It's all mind games. Countless others have made it and so can I."

After the second week, almost half of the class was gone. They had a couple of days of rest where they weren't running around in the woods, but still didn't get any more sleep and instead had some grueling log and rifle PT sessions. Not as many were quitting as when they had first arrived, but each day, one or two more candidates would show up at the cadre's door, knock, and voluntarily withdraw, or VW, from the course.

By the start of the third week, what they were calling SR week, there were 170 candidates left. They were placed into 12 separate teams with 14 or 15 men each. Again, Rourk and Tommy were not together.

After the end of the first day, Rourk found Tommy sitting on his bed taking care of some of the blisters on his feet.

"How'd today go?" Rourk asked as he sat down on Tommy's bunk.

"Ugh, probably about the same as yours. How many guys from your team quit?"

"Three. We started with the ammo crate carry. Within the first two kilometers, the first two VW'd. After lunch and right before we started the second event, the third guy went up to the cadre and VW'd. Left us with an odd number, but gave us an extra rest man."

"My team lost five. What the hell? I can't say it didn't cross my mind a couple of times while as my grip was giving out that it would be easier to just call it than suffering through this, but I didn't want to let you down. What the hell does SR stand for anyway?"

"Situation, Reaction. Typical military, putting an acronym to everything. Don't think of it as letting me down, think of it as letting yourself down. Look how far we've come already." Rourk moved to the floor and started to stretch a bit. His legs were starting to get stiff sitting on the bunk.

"I know, it's pretty crazy."

At the end of the 24 days, both Rourk and Tommy were standing in formation waiting to hear if their roster number would be called.

"Listen up candidates," the Senior Assessor Cadre addressed them. "If I call your number off, fall out of formation and move into classroom number 2."

The tension and nervousness was in the air as numbers were called out in random order. "17, 64, 311, 224, 152..." In all, twenty-seven numbers of the 133 candidates left were called. Neither Rourk or Tommy's number was called.

After the last candidate that was called had entered into the classroom, the Senior Assessor Cadre looked over the ones that were left. "Congratulations men. You've been successfully selected for further training.

Over half of those standing let out a cheer. Rourk smiled and looked over at Tommy, who had a grin from ear to ear and was shaking the hands of those who stood around him. After they were dismissed, Tommy came over to Rourk and shook his hand.

"We did it!"

"Yes we did. I told you that you would make it."

"Of course, it's not over yet. We still need to find out what our MOS will be, and from there how much longer our training will be." Tommy ran his hand through his hair.

"Do you have a preference?" Rourk glanced over at Tommy.

"I'm hoping for Medic, but I'm not sure if my scores are high enough." Tommy said.

"That's another year of training. I'm hoping for anything, but medic." Rourk laughed. "Where do you want to be stationed?"

"It doesn't really matter to me. What about you?"

"I'm hoping for Washington State, 1st Group."

"Really? Why? It's cold and rainy there man."

"I like cold and rainy." *Not really*. However, for whatever reason Keegan's dream was to go to Alaska. Rourk would really prefer to stay near Tennessee and go to 5th group at Fort Campbell, Kentucky. He only planned on staying the initial four years, and then he would go back to the Army of the Light so it didn't really matter where he lived.

"Tonight, we pick up girls." Tommy slapped Rourk on the back.

"Sure, Tommy. We saw how good that went last time."

Tommy looked down at his bandaged feet. "Let's just grab something to eat and get some sleep. At least we get a couple of weeks of downtime to let our feet heal."

Chapter 22

Thaddeus took a sip of his hot chocolate and looked around the coffee shop before sending Anna a text. *Sorry I've been busy. Can you get away today?*

Her response was immediate, making him roll his eyes. Keegan and her friends were surgically attached to their phones. *Of course. Where do you want to meet?*

Pick me up at the Starbucks near Target.

Now?

In about twenty minutes.

Ok.

Thaddeus grinned. Anna was right, this cloak and dagger stuff was pretty fun.

Anna pulled up out front in her old, beat-up car and Thaddeus chugged the last of his hot chocolate as he walked out the door. He tossed it in the trash can out in front of the store.

It was a cool, sunny day with the kind of warm breeze that heralded spring. Thaddeus was glad it was finally April. Cold weather sucked.

"So where are we going?" Anna looked over at Thaddeus, both of her hands wrapped around the wheel.

Thaddeus eyed her bright blue highlights warily. She was such a weird chick. "To the vault."

"The vault. It sounds so mysterious." She put the car into drive and pulled away from the curb. "Thanks, for letting me in on this, Thad."

"No problem." He didn't want to tell her she was his only option. That might hurt her feelings. He pointed for her to take a left.

"So do you think this will work?"

"I hope so. But as I'm sure you know, there are no guarantees with magic. At least we can say we tried."

"I have to admit. I feel slightly bad for Donald. He's innocent in all of this."

"He'll be ok." Thaddeus shrugged.

"How do you know he'll be ok? Did you have a vision?"

"Maybe."

"You're not going to tell me what it was are you?"

"Nope."

"I wouldn't want your gift, Thaddeus," Anna answered in a quiet voice, shooting a glance over at him.

"No, you wouldn't. It's not as cool as people think."

"Speaking of cool. I think it's pretty awesome you are helping out your sister."

Thaddeus cleared his throat and shifted uncomfortably. "I'm helping Rourk."

"Same thing."

Giving her one of his impish smiles, he said, "Anna, I'm going to have to wipe your memory once we get back. You're not supposed to know where the vault is."

"You can trust me. I would never tell anyone."

"I'm sorry, Anna, you have to agree to that or we can't go any further."

"Fine. But just take away the directions nothing else. I like my memories." She paused. "Most of them anyway." She stole a sideways glance at him, her eyes narrowed. "Can you make my crush on Xavier go away?"

"You wouldn't want that, Anna."

"Yeah, I guess you're right. I don't suppose you can tell me the formula to my prefect match could you?"

"Hmm, that is certainly against the rules," Thaddeus murmured, rubbing his chin in his best evil genius impression. He grinned. "If this plan works, I'll look into it."

"Ack! Are you serious? I was just joking. You could really do that?"

"Sure, it's not that hard."

"I wonder what he looks like, my soulmate?"

"Anna, focus. You are going to turn right up ahead. Drive ten miles and take a left on to a hidden driveway. We are going to have to walk about three miles in the woods." He leaned over, looking down at her feet on the pedals and nodded. "I'm glad you wore comfortable shoes."

Once they arrived, Thaddeus had her park the car just off the driveway and they started through the woods. "You didn't say it was going to be three miles uphill, and it's freezing."

"It's not all uphill and it's definitely not freezing. It's almost sixty degrees. You sound like Keegan." Thaddeus rolled his eyes.

"Fine. Okay, so how is this going to work?"

"Well, you are going to read the Book of Shadows. Find a dream spell, and an enchantment spell. I'll memorize them and write them down once we get back to the coffee shop."

"You can do that?"

"Of course, I have a photographic memory."

"How could I forget? The Great Thaddeus."

"That's me." He came to an abrupt halt, one arm swinging out to stop Anna. "Ok, we're here."

"What do you mean we're here? There is nothing but woods."

Thaddeus just grinned. "Anna, take my hands and close your eyes."

Anna did as he said. Suddenly, she felt like the floor had dropped from under her and her stomach flipped. As quickly as it started, it was over.

"You can open your eyes now."

Anna did, and looked around the room in awe. "This is beautiful. Hey, I thought you were supposed to cloak me or something like that?"

"This was easier. No one will know you are here, and we'll just teleport out."

"So this is the famous vault?" Anna walked forward, Thaddeus at her back as she gazed around the room, taking in as many details as she could.

The walls were a shimmering gold color and home to intricately carved wooden bookcases that held what, by sight, seemed to be thousands upon thousands of books. In the center of the room under high ceilings, several heavy wood tables were spread, some of them already holding opened books beneath softly lit lamps. The vault had the dim, comforting feeling of being underground, and it literally hummed with an energy that tickled Anna's skin.

"Somehow I doubt it's famous. But yes, this is the vault. Pretty cool, huh?"

"I'd say." Anna ran her hands along the jewels that were embedded in the gold walls. There was a variety of colors, catching the lights from the tables so that they sparkled as she moved past them. They looked like a treasure.

"Okay, let's get started." Thaddeus moved to the center of the room and closed his eyes, his hands hanging loosely at his sides.

Anna had a moment where she thought she could see the man he would become one day. She always forgot he was only twelve because he was so much more mature due to his gifts. For just a moment, she saw past the twelve year old and to the person he would be. It was an odd sensation. She'd known him since he was little; the idea of him growing up had never occurred to her.

Opening his eyes, Thaddeus walked to a bookshelf in the left corner and grabbed purposefully for a leather bound book. It was the Book of Shadows.

"How did you do that? Magic?"

"Some would say it's magic, but I just used my photographic memory. So we didn't have to waste a lot of time trying to find the book."

"You're pretty cool, Thad."

"And you're weird." He handed her the thick

black book.

"Thaddeus, it's charged with energy. It completely surrounds it."

"I would hope so." He grinned. "It was someone's magic book at one time."

Staring down at the book between her hands, Anna slowly shook her head. "I can't believe I am touching a real Book of Shadows. One from another witch. I have dreamed of this moment for a very long time. I'm afraid to open it."

Thaddeus reached over and opened the book, putting it on the table in front of them. "There. Now find the passages we need."

Anna rolled her eyes at him for ruining her moment, then closed them and placed both hands on the book. Thaddeus paced around her, his lips pursed as he waited.

"Page 333," Anna said excitedly after a few minutes. "The numbers 333 keep playing over in my head."

"Well, check it out."

Anna flipped ahead in the book, careful not to harm the aged, yellowed pages. "Oh my Goddess, Thaddeus. It is page 333. How cool is that? The enchantment spell." A note of reverence was in her voice. "Thaddeus, we could do so many things with this one spell."

"Anna, don't even think about it. We are here for one reason and one reason only. Do not make me regret bringing you here. You would not like the consequences."

"I'm sorry. You're right. Magic is just so powerful. Okay, so here is the spell. Do you want me to say it aloud or do you need to read it to memorize it?"

"I'll read it." He scanned the page quickly. "Ok, now we need to find the dream spell."

Once again, Anna closed her eyes and placed her hands lightly on the book. "I'm not getting it, Thad."

"Try again and relax your mind."

Anna thought about the way her mind cleared when she sat and watched the sunrise or sunset. Since Magdalena had asked her to do the seven day exercises, Anna had tried to keep up with doing it at least once a week. She found that same peace and stillness inside her, then her eyes popped open. "Page 213. Incredible."

"Hurry up, we can't stay in here too long." Thaddeus tapped his fingers on the long wooden table.

"Ok, here it is, 213. I can't wait to try these out."

"Well, if everything goes as planned you can start the dream spell tonight."

Anna jumped up and down.

"What is it with you guys and always jumping around like fools? You're not three years old."

"Did you memorize it? That's it, Thaddeus, I'm hugging you and you can't get out of it." She slipped her arms under his and picked him up, spinning him around the room. He was a lot heavier than she had expected.

"Put me down," Thaddeus growled.

"Fine. Can you show me the rest of the vault?"

"No. Close your eyes and grab my hands."

Anna had that same feeling as if she was dropping from the sky. When she opened her eyes they were back in her car. "Hey! Why did we have to hike that hill if we could have teleported from the car?"

He grinned. "I missed my workout this morning."

"Ugh. Thanks a lot. My legs are already sore." She smacked him on his shoulder.

"Ok, give me a piece of paper."

Anna grabbed her notebook and handed it to him. He started writing so fast Anna couldn't keep up.

"Ok, here are the spells. I'm not a witch so I don't know everything you are supposed to do. Do you have an altar?"

"Of course."

"Well, I'll just give you the spell and you get a hold of the things you need. If you need any help finding something, send me a text. Don't forget—no one is allowed to know we are doing this. Not even your mom."

"I know, you can trust me. Keegan is my best friend." Anna glanced sideways at him. "So are you going to erase my memory now?"

Thaddeus chuckled. "You are so gullible. I was just messing with you. You couldn't find your way back there if you tried."

Chapter 23

Anna emerged from her bath and blew out the candles. The scent of rosemary, lavender, basil, and mint filled the air. She inhaled deeply, taking in the relaxation of the room. Walking slowly to her altar, she lifted the quartz crystal pendent from where it lay across her wooden pentacle and clasped it around her neck. She reached for her white robe, pulling it on while trying to remain calm and not let her excitement take over.

Her hands were shaking as she grabbed the loose earth she had collected from outside and poured it into her antique crystal bowl. She lightly placed the bowl down so it was facing north, the place of power. She paused, kneeling before the small bowl, dipping the fingers of her power hand into the earth. Magdalena had taught her to take just a moment to attune herself with each element by reflecting on how it had touched her life recently. Earth was stability and knowledge, just as Magdalena had become Anna's stability and an endless source of magical knowledge.

Lifting the censer and a small cone of incense, she placed them to the east, letting the cone rest atop the pile of sand in the censor. She lit a match and the smell of sandalwood filled the room. Inhaling deeply, she let it fill her senses, thinking of the warm winds of spring slowly blowing in as winter faded.

Taking the silver candle from her altar, she lit the wick and placed it to the south next to a moonstone. She kneeled before it, staring into the flame. She thought of how fire was strong and determined, as she was determined to bring Keegan's bond back.

Anna picked up the last element—her small brass cup that was filled with water. Carefully, she carried it and placed it in the western quarter. She swirled a single finger in the liquid, watching the water ripple. Water was an emotional element. It made her think of love.

Seating herself in the center of the circle, Anna lit a single purple pillar candle on the floor in front of her. She lifted both of her arms to the ceiling and closed her eyes, her voice flowing smoothly into the dimness of her room.

> *God and Goddess I ask of thee*
> *Give me the ability to send forth this dream*
> *Across the Earth or water's bound*
> *Whether he be in the sky or on the ground*
> *By the powers of fire let it shine bright*
> *By the powers of the earth and air send it*
> * tonight*
> *By the powers of water to sweep within the*
> * dream's door*

And by the powers of 3 shall Rourk remember it evermore.

Anna kept her eyes closed, focusing on the images she wanted to place in Rourk's mind.

Rourk sat on his bed and stared at the ring. The ruby and diamonds sparkled in the light as he twirled it around his finger. His mother whispered in his ear, "It belongs to Keegan now."

Rourk shot out of bed, his breathing ragged as he swiped his hand across the sweat on his forehead. *It was only a dream.*

It had seemed so real. He couldn't remember the last time he had heard his mother's voice. Rourk ran his hand through his hair. His heart was pounding. He glanced over at the clock to see it was barely past midnight. He hadn't been out very long. Closing his eyes, he tried to will himself to fall asleep.

His father was holding the ruby ring in his hand. Crystalline red prisms of light danced on the walls. "Your mother would want her to have it, son."

Rourk reached for the ring, taking it from his father's hand. "What if she says no?"

"You will never know unless you ask. The ring belongs to her."

Rourk tossed and turned, drifting in and out of consciousness. Each time he awoke, he wondered where the dreams were coming from. They were so lifelike, and he rarely recalled his dreams.

Keegan's face lit up, the ring on her hand glowing with a brilliant light. "I love it! I love it!

Thank you, Rourk." *She threw her arms around him and kissed him, sending electricity through his body.*

Rourk angrily threw off his sheet and jumped out of bed. Wrapping his arms around his waist, he leaned forward, squeezing his eyes shut. He wasn't sure he could take the pain much longer. He missed her so much. The dreams were just another element of torture.

It was useless trying to go back to bed. Stepping into his running shorts, he headed out for a ten mile run.

As if he could run from her.

Anna smiled as she blew out the candle and wondered if it worked. She figured that would be enough for tonight. She planned on sending him dreams for the next three days, and after that once or twice a week. She couldn't believe it could be this simple.

Please, Goddess, let this work.

Chapter 24

He was avoiding sleep as much as possible because every time he closed his eyes, the dreams haunted him. He threw himself into his training and pushed himself as far as he could, trying to push the images out of his head. That damn ring was driving him crazy, and hearing his mother so often made him want to punch something.

There was one point during training they had to go four days without sleep or eating. He started hallucinating scenes with his mother and Keegan. They were spinning around and around with their hands clasped between them. The ruby ring was throwing light around like a disco ball. Rourk tried to get to them, but every time he got close, they disappeared. He was worried he was losing his mind. Although, he knew lack of sleep and food could make a mind do strange things.

He finally gave in and called his father.

"Father, I will need the ring for Keegan's birthday."

"I advised against this." His father's deep, gruff voice came crisply across the line.

"Yes, I know."

"Then, why?"

"I won't know unless I try. The worst she can say is no." Although, Rourk thought, that would be the most terrible thing to ever happen to him if she did.

"How do you know you'll be here for her birthday? What about training?"

"I got selected as weapons specialist so I will have plenty of weekends free. I will be able to make it for her birthday. I would be there even if I had to go AWOL."

"You're a grown man. I won't stand in your way."

"Thanks, Dad." Rourk hung up the phone. He was exhausted, but he still fought sleep as long as he could. Eventually, when he drifted off, his mother came to him again.

"You did the right thing son. You know the ring belongs to her."

Rourk woke up and he could have sworn he felt his mother brush his hair to the side. He was losing it.

Rourk wasn't sure what happened, but that was the last dream he had about the ring. He was relieved; his body needed the rest.

He couldn't wait to see Keegan again, even if she did turn him down. He knew he had to ask her. That is what chosens did. He had told her he was coming back for her on her birthday and he wasn't about to break that promise.

He didn't get to see Tommy as much, because he got picked up for the engineer program. Rourk got selected for the weapons slot which was fine by him. The training was much shorter, and they had a lot more freedom to do what they wanted. They had their own rooms, and were able to come and go as they pleased as long as they didn't miss training. The training was fun for Rourk. He loved guns and he got to shoot a lot. He figured Tommy was having a good time learning how to blow up things.

When they got their duty stations, Rourk was surprised that Tommy also got 1st Group in Washington State.

"That is pretty crazy. I'm sorry you didn't get 5th Group like you wanted."

"I actually requested 1st. I figured if you could put up with rain and cold, so could I."

Rourk gave his friend a big smile. "I'm glad, Tommy. Maybe we will even get on the same team."

"That's what I'm hoping." Tommy grinned.

"Mom, I'm going to get the girls. We're going to look for our prom dresses." Keegan reached over her mom and grabbed a chip from the bag on the table.

"I thought I was going to take you?" Keegan had never seen her mom pout before.

"Sorry, I'll text you the pics and you can help me decide."

"Ok, don't forget."

"I won't." Keegan kissed her mom and headed out the door.

Summer was quickly approaching. Keegan decided to take down the top to her Jeep before she went to get her friends. After two seconds trying, she realized what a pain it was to do it alone and ran back inside the house.

Her mother was still at the table. Keegan smiled sweetly. "Mom, can you help me take the top down?"

"Sure, give me a second." She slipped on her shoes and headed out.

With the two of them doing it, they got the top down in record time and Keegan slid in to the driver's seat, cranking the engine.

"Don't forget to send me the pictures," her mom yelled as Keegan pulled out of the driveway. Keegan waved an arm to show she had heard her.

She loved the breeze against her skin and the sun beating down on her bare shoulders. She cranked up the radio and sang along on the drive, navigating the roads with ease.

Keegan stopped at Lauren's first. Lauren ran out in a yellow tank top, cut-off jean shorts, and flip flops. She pouted as she hopped in the passenger seat and slammed the door behind her. "Ah Keegan, my hair is going to get messed up."

"Stop being a baby." Keegan reached over and popped open the glove box, pulling out a bandana. "Here, put this on till we get to the mall."

"Fine." Lauren pulled down the mirror while she pushed her mass of curls under the bandana. "I actually look pretty cute."

"You always look beautiful," Keegan answered, signaling as she turned off of Lauren's street. "Now, let's get Anna. I'm so excited she actually wanted to go shopping with us."

"I know. I think she's sad we are all going to be moving soon for college," Lauren said loudly over the sound of the wind in the car.

The thought of it subdued Keegan, as well. "It is sad! You'll be in California, I'll be in Alaska, and Anna will be in Seattle. At least we'll all be on the west coast. I'm sure we'll manage to get together often."

"I hope so. Although, don't plan on me visiting you too often in Alaska. I have no idea why you want to go to that frozen tundra."

"It has a great marine biology program."

"So does California, and you don't have to freeze to death."

They pulled into Anna's driveway and she came bouncing out. She was dressed pretty mild today with a black T-shirt and a black tutu skirt. She had black flats on her feet and streaks of red in her hair.

"You make us look so boring." Lauren turned in the seat to stick her tongue out at Anna.

"Can we stop at Starbucks on the way? I'm in need of caffeine," Anna said as she vaulted the side of the Jeep and plopped into the backseat.

"You won't get any arguments from us," Keegan told her, aiming for the nearest Starbucks.

Once they got to the mall with coffee cups in hand, they chose to check out the dresses at Macy's first.

"I know short dresses are in, but I really want to wear a long dress to prom. That's been my vision of prom since I was a little girl." Wrinkling her nose, Keegan put the short purple dress she was holding back on the rack.

"Good luck finding one." Anna spread her hands out at the sea of short dresses in front of them.

"Plus, you're so short you're going to have to get it tailored big time." Lauren fingered a shimmering blue dress. "Let's just try on some of the short ones first. If you still want a long dress we'll search the whole mall if we have to. What do you think of this one?" Lauren held up the short strapless dress with scrunching and fake gems she had been eyeing.

Keegan glanced over. "For you? I don't think so. You have that athletic straight figure, so you want to make it appear that you have curves. You know, an optical illusion."

"Shut up, Keegan. I'm not that straight. We can't all have a J-Lo booty like you." She pouted, putting the dress back.

Keegan grabbed a black strapless number that flared out at the waist, and had a purple ribbon around the waist, shoving it in Lauren's hands. "Here try this one on."

"It's so plain."

"Just try it on."

Lauren stepped out of the dressing room, and spun around. "Keegan, how do you know this stuff? It's perfect."

"That really does look good. What dress do you think would look good on me?" Anna asked.

Keegan looked Anna up and down. "You can really wear anything. It's gotta be funky to match your style. Oh, what about this?" She picked up an all black lacy dress with ruffles. "It's so vintage looking."

"That's cute, but I kinda like this one." Anna showed them an off-the-shoulder teal dress that had a flowing top and ruffles on the bottom.

"You do? That doesn't look like your style at

all. Try them both on." Keegan pushed her in the dressing room.

A few minutes later she came out in the all black dress and the girls cooed about how great it looked. Lauren clapped her hands together and said, "Go try on the teal one. I can't wait to see it on you."

When she emerged a couple moments later, both Lauren and Keegan gasped.

"Wow, Anna, you look amazing. You're right. You have to go with that one." Keegan snapped a picture.

Keegan grabbed a few dresses and tried them on. She could try on clothes all day. She loved them all, but nothing felt like the one. So they moved on to the next store.

Three stores later, when they were about to give up, Keegan's phone chirped in her pocket. *Where are my pictures?*

"Ugh, guys I forgot to send my mom pictures. Let's go to the next shop we see and try some on and I'll go to another mall later with my mom."

"What about that store?" Anna pointed to a bridal shop.

"That's a wedding shop." Lauren looked at Anna like she was crazy.

"Yeah, but they have colorful gowns. Let's just go try some on, it might be fun."

"Sure, why not?" Keegan laced her arms between theirs and they headed to the store.

The sales lady must have been bored or in need of a sale, because she treated them like royalty. She ran around, grabbing gowns for them to try on and shoving them over the top of the dressing rooms.

The girls walked their self-made runway, twirling around and posing dramatically. The sales woman seemed to be having as much fun as they were. They snapped tons of pictures to send to Keegan's mother.

"Ok, Keegan, you were right. Long gowns are so much cooler. I vote we take back these short dresses and get long ones." Lauren spun around in a hot pink a-line gown with glitter all over.

"As long as you promise you are not going to buy that one!" Keegan was laughing so hard her eyes were watering.

"I didn't mean this one." Lauren rolled her eyes. "We need to start looking seriously instead of just playing around."

"I'm not taking back my dress. I'll find somewhere else to wear it. I will get a long gown, though. I hope we're the only ones with long gowns. We'll really stand out." Anna grinned.

Keegan flung the curtain open and came out in a strapless silver mermaid dress that clung to her curves and sashayed down the walkway.

"Oh my god! Keegan, that dress is stunning. It looks like it was made just for you." Lauren took a picture with her phone.

"She's right, this is the one you have been looking for. Do you love it?"

Keegan's face beamed. "It's perfect!"

"I love how it has the drop waist to show off your booty, and your tiny waist." Anna laughed. "Spin around again. Oooh, it even has the corset lace in the back. You have to get this one."

"Send a picture to my mom."

Anna laughed. "Your mom replied back 'wrap it up.'"

"Yay! Okay, let's find dresses for both of you now."

"Oh, I forgot we just got a shipment in," the clerk said quickly, snapping her fingers. "One minute. I think I might have the perfect dress for both of you." She hurried to the back of the store.

She came out holding a long black gown with polka dots, and a few others in various styles and colors.

Anna grabbed the polka dotted dress. "I call this one."

She disappeared into the dressing room. She popped out in the strapless gown, laughing as she spun in a circle. "I love this one! Take my picture and send it to my mom."

It was simple and beautiful at the same time. A small dark pink belt was wrapped around the waist, and the bottom of the dress flared out in the front shorter than it was in the back.

"Okay, now I have to find something," Lauren said. "What else do you have in that pile?"

Lauren tried on two that were okay, but not perfect.

Keegan eyed the substantial pile of dresses they'd built up. Digging one out from underneath, she handed it to Lauren. "Here try this one."

Lauren came out in the plum colored, one-shoulder taffeta gown. The color was striking against her alabaster skin and dark hair.

"Oh, this is the one," Keegan squealed. "You look so curvy in it."

"I look curvy? Well, if I look curvy, I'll take it!" Lauren declared, making her friends laugh.

Anna nodded, reaching out to touch the soft material. "It's very glamorous."

Lauren turned side to side, checking herself out in the mirror. "It's beautiful, isn't it?"

"Yes, it is. Strike a pose." Keegan waited for Lauren to turn then snapped a photo.

"Would you guys like me to take a picture of all three of you?" the clerk offered.

"Oh, that would be great." Keegan handed her the camera. *I wonder if I should add this picture to Rourk's scrapbook?*

Since Christmas, when her family had suggested she take pictures for Rourk, she had been gathering some in a small scrapbook. Eventually, she would send it to him. She just never felt the time was right.

"Should we look for accessories now?" Lauren asked as they left the store with their purchased dresses in hand.

"I'm too tired. We'll have to do that another day." Anna shifted the dress to her other arm and sighed. "Shopping is exhausting. I don't know how you guys love it so much."

"Whatever, you had fun and you know it," Keegan teased, poking her in the side.

"I did have fun. Can you believe we will be graduating soon? It's kinda scary. Soon our lives are going to be so different."

"I'm excited about the changes. I can't wait." Lauren hugged her dress closer and smiled.

"We have to promise to get together as often as possible. We also have to Skype."

"Agreed."

After Keegan dropped them off at their houses, she turned towards home and thought of how much fun she and her friends had together over the years. She smiled wistfully, wishing it didn't have to change.

Chapter 25

"Mom my hair is a mess!" Keegan wailed, staring forlornly in the antique vanity mirror. She lifted her hands to her head, but Emerald swatted them away.

"It's not a mess. It looks beautiful. You look beautiful. You'll be the most gorgeous girl at prom." Her mother tugged at a curl and laughed as it sprang back up. "I love when you wear your hair curly. It looks natural and wild, just like you."

"Do you really think I look okay?" Keegan stared at her mother's reflection in the mirror. Her mother's smile was beautiful.

"More than okay, Keegan. You are a striking young woman. Stand up so I can see the dress." Emerald gestured with both hands for her daughter to move.

Keegan slowly rose from her chair, brushing her palms nervously down the front of her silver gown. It made her feel feminine.

Conflicted

"Spin around. You know you want to."

Keegan laughed and spun. "It is the perfect dress."

"I'm sure your father will say it's too perfect. It really accents your curves. You are definitely not a little girl anymore." Emerald sighed. "Makes me sad, in a way. However, I'm also looking forward to the next stage in your life. You're going to do great things, I know."

"Mom, I'm nervous to move so far away from you guys."

"I know, honey, I'm nervous too. Who is going to cook for you?" Her mother gave a sad laugh and looked away. "Thank goodness for the internet. We will stay in touch. I can always come see you in Alaska when I need my Keegan fix. Of course, you will come home for the holidays I would hope."

"Of course." Keegan dabbed at her eyes with an old t-shirt and sniffed. "Okay, let's change the subject before you ruin my makeup."

"Donald is picking you up right?"

"Yes. I'm sure he will look great all dressed up. He's already so cute."

Her daughter's dreamy eyes made Emerald nervous. She rubbed her face with one hand then looked into Keegan's eyes. "Keegan, I really hate to ask you this, but I know a lot of kids have sex on prom night. Do I need to be worried? Or get you some protection?"

"What? No, mom. I'm not ready for that. It hasn't even crossed my mind. I still have the 'wait for your chosen' mentality, I guess." Keegan looked down and moved her brush around the vanity, surprised she wasn't embarrassed by her mother's blunt question.

Keegan could see how relieved her mom was to hear her answer. "I'm glad to hear that. If you change your mind, please let me know. I know that your situation is different from most. If you feel you are ready, I'll take you to the doctor and get you on birth control. I don't want to be a grandmother just yet."

"I will, Mom." Keegan leaned over and gave her mom a quick hug. "Thanks for helping me get ready for prom."

"Let's go show the boys how fabulous you look." Emerald took her daughter's hand, tugging her towards the door

"Wait, I almost forgot the mask." Keegan grabbed the mask from her bookshelf. It was a very dramatic looking mask. Meant only to rest over her eyes and cheekbones, it had cat-shaped eyes with spiraling lace that feathered from the corner of each. The base of the mask was burnished gold and covered in intricate black designs. A single small hoop rose from the top of the mask like the crown of a tiara.

As they walked down the stairs, Keegan holding her mother's arm for support, Emerald yelled, "Check out the princess!"

Her father looked up from his Macbook when they rounded the corner into the living room. "I think you need to go back up and change into something that doesn't make you look so...what is the word I'm looking for?" Keegan's face fell as he paused, but he rubbed his beard and grinned. "Just kidding. You look wonderful, Keegan. It's hard for me to see you so grown up."

"Dad, I'm almost eighteen. You need to let go

of the little girl image you have of me."

"Never," he said with a smile.

"What do you think, Thaddeus?" Keegan glanced over at her brother.

He was sprawled across the love seat, his feet propped up on one arm and a book open across his chest. Raising an eyebrow, he answered, "You look ugly. However, I'm sure you already know that with your big ego."

"Funny." Keegan swatted him on the shoulder.

"Ouch. Did you see that mom?"

The doorbell rang and the four of them yelled in unison, "Come in."

"Hey!" Donald called as the front door clicked open. A second later, he appeared in the archway between the foyer and the living room. His tux was black and the vest peeking through the jacket was the exact silver of Keegan's dress.

When his bright blue eyes landed on Keegan standing in the middle of the room, he stared. "Wow." He paused, unable to find any more words, and blushed when the rest of the family laughed. "Sorry, that's all I can think to say."

"Thaddeus, go grab my camera," Emerald said. "Let's get some photos of these two together."

They spent the next twenty minutes taking photos, some nice and posed and a few goofy ones added at the end for good measure. Keegan smiled thinking about how someday she would look back at the photos and recall a wonderful moment in her life. Photography was the greatest invention.

"Ok, we really need to get out of here,"

Keegan said, waving at her family as she took her boyfriend's arm. "Come on, Donald. Bye guys, don't wait up."

Richard cleared his throat and stood, looming menacingly over the two of them. "Donald, just because it's prom night don't get any ideas in your head."

"Of course not. I respect your daughter. You have made it clear as long as she is living under your roof..."

"If I had my way, I'd lock her up until she was thirty," Richard said gruffly, scowling.

Keegan rolled her eyes. "Bye!"

Her mother yelled out the door as they left. "You forgot your mask."

Keegan let go of Donald and ran back inside to grab it. "Thank you. I'd be lost without you."

"Yes, you would." Emerald chuckled.

Donald held the door open to his mother's sedan. He gave her a lopsided grin. "I borrowed the good car."

After she was settled, he walked around and got in on the driver's side. In the silence before he started the car, he said softly, "Keegan, you are too stunning for words."

"Don't make me blush," she replied, her cheeks already heated. Giving him a sideways glance, she said, "You look pretty sexy yourself in that tux. I noticed you couldn't go without the Chucks. I like it."

"Thanks."

They stared at each other a moment longer before they met in the middle of the car for a deep kiss. He wrapped one of her curls around his finger as she slid her hands across the smooth fabric of his suit jacket. Keegan felt flushed when he finally pulled away, her lips warm. "Let's get to the hotel before we miss all the fun."

Keegan was impressed that they could turn a boring room into a beautiful space for a masquerade ball. Lauren, who had worked tirelessly on the prom committee, must have aimed to make sure everything was perfect.

As she and Donald walked through the door, confetti was thrown over them and Keegan laughed in delight. They entered beneath an arch of purple, gold, and black balloons with a large, hand painted sign that read "Masquerade" in swirly letters.

From the ceiling of the ballroom, purple and black sheer cloth draped elegantly, framing a beautiful chandelier of cut glass that was dimmed enough to only cast a little light on the dance floor. Tables of students spread around the area where other kids mingled or danced.

The band was playing a slow song so she pulled Donald straight to the dance floor.

"This is amazing." Keegan laid her head against his chest.

"Yes, it really is. This has been the best school year for me. I almost wish it didn't have to end."

"I know what you mean." Keegan pulled him a little tighter.

After the song was over, Keegan said, "I need to find the girls so I can see them in their dresses."

"Sure, I'll go find the guys and we can meet up in about half an hour."

Keegan gave him a quick kiss and hurried off

in search of them. People kept stopping her to tell her how much they loved her dress, which made her glow with pride. She finally saw Lauren and Anna together near the punch table.

"Someone spiked the punch." Anna handed a cup to Keegan.

"Awesome. It was probably Spencer or Calvron." They laughed and downed their drinks. The fruity liquid had a strong taste of alcohol.

"Where are your dates?" Keegan asked. The two of them had accepted invitations from two guys from their class.

Anna giggled, grabbing the spoon and refilling Keegan's cup as she held it out. "We ditched them."

"You ditched them? Why?"

"Because they were lame."

Lauren nodded her agreement, her face hidden behind her cup.

"I guess that's a good reason. Give me another."

When they all had another drink in hand, Keegan raised her paper cup. "To us magical creatures."

The tapped their cups and downed the liquid.

"Whoa, this stuff is strong." Anna giggled.

"You're cut off." Lauren took her cup.

Keegan put an arm around both of their shoulders. "You guys are great. So are you having fun? You both look gorgeous."

"Sure, if you call standing by yourself in the corner drinking spiked punch fun," Lauren mumbled.

"Well let's get out there and dance." Keegan grabbed them and started pulling them along.

"Hey, I wanted another drink," Anna complained.

"Lauren cut you off. Come on."

They spent the evening dancing, laughing, and having a great time. Eventually, the guys joined them. Everyone cleared a spot for Lauren and Donald to have a dance off. It was a riot.

After the prom, they all congregated outside in the parking lot.

"Calvron, I think you should make a magical land for us to hang out in for the evening," Keegan said, looking over at him expectantly.

Only Calvron could pull off the blindingly white tuxedo with a baby blue shirt. His shoes had pointy toes that made Keegan giggle. He tapped his chin thoughtfully. "That's a great idea. It will take me a little while. Let's all head over to the location and I can get started."

"Yay!" Keegan gazed up into Donald's eyes, smiling. "This will be a prom to remember, that's for sure."

"It's ready!" Calvron yelled an hour later, his voice drifting over from the darkness beyond the light of the headlights.

Keegan and Donald had been sitting on the tailgate of Calvron's truck, chatting with the others. It was the kind of humid Tennessee night that made Keegan want to stay outside forever and the companionship of her friends made her nostalgic for it to never end.

She squealed when she saw the glass double-doors. Calvron had outdone himself, as usual. He had made three distinct setups. One was an old fashioned diner: cooks, waiters and all surrounded by red pleather booths and checkered tablecloths. Another section was a disco center with flashing lights and music that could only be heard when you crossed into the area. The third was a relaxing coffee shop; it even smelled like one.

Keegan skipped over to give Calvron a hug. "This is perfect!"

"I'm starving, let's eat first," Anna said, heading for the diner.

The rest of them followed after her. Keegan marveled at the stainless steel area. She ran her hand across the vinyl table and sat down on the red seat. She laughed when it squeaked under her weight.

The waitress sidled up to the table, dressed in a gray, cotton dress with her name—Pattie—stitched at the breast. Her hair was bright blonde and wrapped up in a high bun. She had on inches of makeup and bright red lipstick.

"I'll take the works!" Keegan told her. "Eggs, bacon, toast, potatoes with cheese, and some coffee."

"Sure thing, sweetie. What about the rest of you?" Her voice was deep and hoarse. She cracked her gum, staring at them.

"What she said," Anna answered, handing her menu over to the woman. There was unanimous agreement as everyone ordered the same thing.

"So, it's almost time to graduate," Lauren said with a sigh, adding cream from the pitcher to her coffee.

"It's about time," Sam joked, nudging Spencer, who nodded.

"I think it's sad." Keegan stirred her coffee, watching the sweetener dissolve instead of letting her friends see the tears in her eyes.

"We'll stay in touch," Calvron told her, reaching over to lay a hand on her arm.

Donald slipped his own arm around her shoulders, squeezing her to the side of his body. "Of course we will."

The food was delicious. Keegan ended up having another plate, as did the boys.

After eating, they decided to go hang out in the disco room. When they walked through the door, their outfits changed. Keegan cracked up laughing. Calvron had a huge afro and the guys had on bell bottoms and long sleeved, collared shirts with the buttons undone. The girls, of course, looked hot in their mini skirts and platform shoes.

They danced beneath the disco lights for what seemed like hours, even though they'd already danced most of the night away at prom. When they were sweaty and tired, they made their way to the coffee shop to rest and relax.

Dinner had been great, and the disco crazy, but the most enjoyable thing for Keegan was the time they spent over their coffee, reminiscing about the past.

Chapter 26

Keegan's stomach was in knots. She didn't expect to be this nervous; it was only a high school graduation after all. All she had to do was walk across the stage and smile while she shook the principal's hand. She smoothed down her gown and reached up to make sure the cap was in place, waiting for her name to be called.

"Keegan Clarke," was announced over the loud speaker and her heart skyrocketed.

Taking a deep breath, she walked forward and prayed she didn't fall and make a fool of herself. She had worn ballet flats under the gown to reduce the risk.

She made it across the stage, smiling all the while, and shook the principal's hand. There was a slight awkward moment when she tried to shake with the wrong hand. She always messed that up because she was left handed. Everyone in the crowd laughed. The rest of the ceremony passed in a blur.

Once off the stage, she ran over to Anna and Lauren. "Eeek! I can't believe we graduated." They wrapped their arms around each other, face to face in a big group hug, and bounced up and down.

"I know it's so crazy. We're going to be at college, out on our own in just a couple of months." Lauren sighed and smiled.

"I'm sad high school is over. I don't think I'm ready to move on to college." Anna crossed her arms across her chest.

"You'll be fine. You are going to an awesome art school and you'll meet all kinds of cool people."

"I know, but I'm going to miss you guys." Anna wiped a tear away.

"Don't even start crying. This is supposed to be a happy time. If you cry, we'll all cry," Keegan said.

"That's right, no crying until we board our planes to the new adventures that await us." Lauren looked at Anna and smiled slightly as she wiped away a tear herself.

"Let's go find the boys. That will keep us from being all sappy and emotional." Lauren encircled her arms with theirs as they headed over to find the guys.

Donald, Spencer, and Sam were chasing each other around the gymnasium—big surprise there. Keegan smiled as she saw Donald sneak up behind Spencer. Those guys were clowns. She knew it was going to be hard for them to be separated. She didn't even know where they had decided to go to school. She would have to ask once they finished playing.

"Okay, well they are occupied. Want to go see if there is anything to eat?" Keegan asked.

"I did see some cake when we walked in." Anna grinned.

On their way to find the food, their parents caught up with them. "You didn't think you could sneak off without us taking some photos did you?" Anna's mother shooed them together.

The girls made funny faces and threw up the peace sign.

"You guys will miss this," Lauren's mother said wistfully.

"We're done with the mushy talk, Mom."

"Alright, well go have fun with your friends," Emerald sighed, packing her own camera away. "Don't forget we have to go to the family dinner tonight."

"Thanks for the reminder." Keegan waved as they walked away.

They found the cake and waited in line. There wasn't much in the manner of food other than cake, chips, and soda.

Keegan had her cake up to her mouth when Donald came around and ate it right out of her hand. "Hey! You know, now you have to get in line and get me another piece of cake."

"I'll get you two." He gave her a big grin, the corners of his eyes crinkling. Keegan leaned forward, giving him a peck on the lips.

"You guys are sickening." Lauren rolled her eyes at them.

"Where are you guys going to college?" Keegan asked Calvron and Spencer after Donald had left for the cake table.

"We're going to UCLA. Donald was supposed

to go as well, but I hear he might be going to Alaska instead." Calvron stared intently at her.

"What, you guys were supposed to go to college together? He never told me that." Keegan's mind was racing. Donald was going to give up going to college with his best friends to be closer to her. She really didn't like that idea at all. She knew she wouldn't give up her plans for him.

"I'll talk to him about it later. I really had no idea." Keegan pulled at the sleeve of her gown.

"I didn't know you guys were going to UCLA. That's where I'm going, as well. To study law." Lauren smiled sweetly at them. "We'll have to hang out sometimes."

"Well, that sucks. You guys are going to be together, and Keegan and I are going to be off on our own." Anna shot Lauren a dirty look.

"Hey, you guys picked your schools, I had nothing to do with it."

"We should make plans to meet up once a month," Keegan cut in. "Maybe Calvron can set up a magical world there.

Calvron stroked his chin. "I'm sure I could work something out."

Donald strolled back up to group and handed Keegan her cake. "What did I miss?"

"We were just talking about getting together once a month after we leave for college," Anna told him, stealing a bite from Keegan's plate.

"That would be cool." Donald put his arm around Keegan.

"Ok guys, this graduation is lame. Any idea of what we can do?" Keegan looked around at the gang.

"Let's go play laser tag." Sam grinned.

The girls looked at each other and shrugged their shoulders. "Sure, why not."

They had a blast. The guys were surprised the girls were able to hold their own. Keegan was going to miss days like this.

Chapter 27

Donald and Keegan had just walked outside to go swimming in the natural swimming pool at her house. The day was bright and hot, the sun sparkling off the water as they dropped their towels on one of the tables surrounding the pool.

Keegan turned to stare up into his startling blue eyes. "Donald, why didn't you tell me that you were supposed to go to college in California with the guys?"

"Keegan, I want to be with you. If you're going to Alaska, that's where I want to be." He looked down at her sincerely as he took her hands.

"I think you should go to UCLA. It's not good to change your plans like that. We can take turns visiting each other once or twice a month. Plus, I'm going to be so busy with school, I wouldn't have much time for you anyway."

"Are you saying you don't want me to go?" Donald pulled his hands away from her, his lips pressing into a thin line.

"It's not that I don't want you around, you know I do. It's just, I think you should be with your friends. We can make it work. Besides, what if I hate Alaska and you are stuck there finishing up your program?"

"I could always switch, same as you."

"I'm asking you to do this for me, Donald. Please, just go to UCLA. I promise I will visit you a lot. I feel horrible taking you away from your plans."

"But, it's what I want. I want to be with you. I don't care where it is. I love you."

Keegan was starting to get mad. She wrapped her arms around herself and rubbed her arms, taking a few deep breaths.

Donald noticed and said. "Ok, Keegan if that is really what you want. But, I want to see you every weekend not just two times a month."

"We can try." She smiled and threw her arms around him. "Thank you. I feel so much better now. It has been eating away at me."

"Let's spend as much time as we can together for the rest of the summer."

Keegan laid her head against his chest, relieved. She wasn't sure why it bothered her so much that he was willing to give everything up for her.

Later that day, Anna showed up. "Hey, is Thaddeus around? I have to ask him something about the Xbox."

"You want to see my brother?" Keegan looked at her in disbelief. "I thought you came to hang out with me."

"Don't be ridiculous, of course I did. I just

have to see him for a second."

"Well, he's in his room."

Anna walked up the stairs with a smile on her face, still tickled by the cloak and dagger stuff. She knocked on the door and Thaddeus yelled, "Come in, Anna."

"Hey, how did you know? Oh right never mind." She gave him a sheepish grin. "Well, part one is over. I've been feeding him dreams and if he's going to give her the ring, he would have decided by now. But, we didn't think of the tricky part."

"What's that?" Thad looked up from his game, pausing it.

"We need to get a hold of the ring."

"Ah, yes that is tricky. Well, we can ask his father for it," Thaddeus said.

"Wouldn't that be a little strange? Hey, do you happen to have a ruby ring we could spell?" Anna put her hand on her hip and raised an eyebrow.

"Just leave it to me. I'll get you the ring. When do you need it by?"

"Well, summer is almost over. I need it before I leave for college, because I'm not sure I'll be back here again before her birthday."

"Okay, I'll get it to you by this weekend. I'll figure something out. Where there is magic, there is always a way." He gave her one of his impish grins.

"If Keegan asks, I was asking you about a zombie game."

"Okay, get out of here. Don't forget to shut the door."

Once the door was closed, Thaddeus sat back

in his chair to think. How could he get the ring? He could use magic, of course, but maybe he didn't have to. He picked up his phone and called Rourk's dad. He didn't have to say much to get him to agree to help out. He wanted Rourk to be happy and didn't care how that happened.

Anna and Keegan were watching sappy chick flicks and eating popcorn.

Keegan told Anna about talking Donald into going to school in California.

"I think that's a good idea. It's a little strange he wanted to follow you to Alaska. Even as much as I love you, I have no desire to follow you to Alaska." They both laughed.

Summer passed by in a blur. They all spent as much time together as possible, but it was rapidly coming to an end.

They decided to have one big party before they all went their separate ways. Calvron held it at his house since his family had so much room.

The girls came through the door and were shocked at how many people were there. There had to be over two hundred kids dancing and yelling. They made their way over to the guys.

"Calvron, did you use magic to pull this together?" Keegan wondered aloud.

"Nope, my parents don't let me use magic at home."

"Well, it looks amazing." Anna said as she glanced around the large open room.

"We have a pool out back and some pool tables if you guys want to go back there."

"Sure sounds fun. We didn't bring swim suits

237

though." Lauren shrugged.

"Who said you needed suits." Calvron winked.

"Gross, you wish." Lauren swatted at him.

"There are actually a bunch of suits out there. My parents keep lots on hands for guest."

They had a great time. No one mentioned it was the last time they would hang out like that for a while, even though Keegan figured it was on everyone's mind.

The ring shimmered on Anna's altar under the glow of the circle of candles surrounding her. Her heartbeat was a quick pulse in her throat as she touched a single fingertip to it, closing her eyes and searching for the power inside it. It made her skin tingle.

Taking a deep breath, she released it, imagining a brilliant white light surrounding her body as she rested her hands back in her lap. She let everything else fade away—everything that had bugged her during the day melted under the positive energy. She took a couple of breaths to center herself before she began.

The picture she had of Keegan was a great one. Anna had captured it while she wasn't looking. It was her profile, with her auburn hair tucked behind one ear and dangling on the other side. The sun was behind her, making her hair a halo of fire. A small smirk was on her lips. Anna couldn't remember what she was looking at in the photo, but it had amused her.

Anna put the photo on top of her stone pentacle on the altar, face up. She lifted the ring, eyeing it once more in the candlelight before sitting it on the picture.

She began folding the corners of the picture in one by one, taking her time to make them meet in the center, while she chanted,

In the name of my lady and her consort,
And by the law of three times three,
Let this ring draw Keegan to wear it,
So from darkness she shall be free.

She repeated the chant three times, securing the picture-made envelope that held the ring with a black ribbon. When it was ready, she placed it purposefully back on top of her pentacle.

The candle holder was an antique Anna had pulled from the attic. It was gold but had lost its shine a long time before. Its greatest aspect was the hollow base, which allowed her to position the holder over her pentacle and the talisman.

The pale pink pillar candle she had already anointed with cinnamon oil. The smell was divine and made her want cookies. She fit it in the shallow dish of the holder and lit the candle.

Lighting her sage bundle, she blew gently on it to make it smolder and smoke, then wafted it around her altar in the shape of a heart three times. She put it in the censor dish on her altar to burn out. Clapping her hands once to signal the end of the ritual, she declared, "Blessed be."

She would burn the candle for 13 minutes every night after sunset for 13 days to push the spell. Raising an eyebrow at her handiwork, she smiled. "Now, to see if it works."

Keegan's mother wanted them to get to Alaska a few days early so they could set up her new room. She had decided to get an apartment right outside of the college instead of staying in the dorms. For some reason, her father was very relieved by this. She might get a roommate just so she didn't have to be alone. At the very least she was getting a dog. She still couldn't believe she was going to be so far from home.

"Keegan, are you ready to go?" her mother yelled up the stairs.

"No, I'm not ready."

"Well, we have to leave in a few minutes or we will miss the plane."

Keegan glanced around her childhood room and wanted to crawl back in the bed and stay there. She was actually scared to be going to a strange place all by herself. She didn't want to tell her parents that, though. Taking a deep breath, she picked up her bags and headed out the door.

"Hurry up!"

"I'm coming, stop rushing me!" Keegan ran down the stairs.

Her father and Thaddeus, who were going to drop them off at the airport, were waiting at the door. Thaddeus grabbed her bags from her, which surprised her.

Once they got to the airport, her father hugged her for a long time. Keegan wiped tears from her eyes.

"Stop crying, Keegan, you will be back next month for your birthday. After that, for Thanksgiving and Christmas." Thaddeus looked down at his feet.

"You know you're going to miss me, little

brother."

"Maybe a little bit." He gave her a slight smile.

"Ok, let's go Keegan," her mother said. "I'm excited to get there and get your apartment set up. We have a lot of shopping to do."

Keegan smiled—shopping was the magic word. "I really want my place to be cool. I was thinking to go for the retro look. I hope they have good stores there."

"Well, I wouldn't count on that but we'll make do." Her mother put her arm around her as they walked towards the gate.

"Thanks for coming with me mom."

"I wouldn't miss it."

Keegan had settled into a routine. Thankfully, her earliest class was at 9:00 am so she got to sleep in. She had started volunteering at the fish and wildlife service where she made a few friends, but nothing that came close to her friends from Tennessee. Donald had already come to visit twice. She loved showing him around. They had fun going hiking, fishing, and whale watching. She couldn't believe how cold it got so quickly there.

She kept in constant contact with Anna and Lauren by text and Skype. They seemed to be adjusting well to their new schools, but they were all looking forward to returning to Tennessee for Keegan's birthday party.

Chapter 28

Rourk boarded the plane, nervous anticipation racing through his body.

Soon, he would see Keegan again. It had been almost a year since he had laid eyes on her. He had no idea what her reaction would be when she saw him.

Leaning his head against the seat, he closed his eyes and thought of her. Of course, all he could see was darkness. He longed for the days when he could close his eyes and see her face clearly. That seemed like a lifetime ago.

He was trying to mentally brace himself for her rejection. He hoped he would be able to hold himself together. Noticing that he was gripping the seat tightly, he released his fingers. Thankfully, it was a short flight home.

When he got off the plane, his father was there to meet him. It was nice to see a familiar face in the sea of strangers.

"Rourk, you look great," his father said,

shaking his hand.

"Thanks, Dad. How have you been?"

"I've been well. Let's get you home so you can cook me something to eat. I'm surprised I haven't wasted away without your cooking skills."

Rourk laughed. "That sounds good. I'm so sick of the mess hall food."

He tossed his bag in the back of his father's truck and settled into the passenger seat for the drive home. The familiar highway felt good. To Rourk, Tennessee would always be home, no matter where he lived.

"So you still want to give Keegan the ring?" his father asked, never taking his eyes off the road.

"Yes, I am going to give it to her." Rourk paused, then gave a wry grin. "Well, I'm going to try to give it to her. She might turn me down."

"I've been thinking about it, and I'm glad you are going to try. You are right. You are an elf and that is what chosens do."

Rourk was slightly surprised by his father's change in opinion, but he let it slide.

"I will know soon enough." Rourk relaxed his posture and leaned his head back on the seat.

"How is training going?"

"It's going good. There are some good guys there. I've noticed a few other creatures of the light. The training is actually fun now that it's mostly just weapons and less of the mind games."

"How's Tommy?"

Rourk smiled. "He is doing good. He has really taken to the engineer program. He's actually a very intelligent man. We're both going to 1st Group."

"That is great. Some of my best friends I met as a team guy. I should probably look some of them up now that I think of it," his father mused, his eyes far away.

At home, Rourk cooked steaks and potatoes. It was nice to navigate his kitchen again, and he couldn't wait to sleep in his own bed.

It took all of his self control not to go over to Keegan's house. He knew he had to wait till tomorrow. His pulse quickened at the thought.

Rourk went for a run in his woods and enjoyed the crisp fall air against his skin. Once he got home, he jumped in the shower let the hot water wash away the tension. He wondered if he should call Thaddeus and find out what Keegan's plans were so he knew when the best time to visit would be.

Wrapping a towel around his waist, Rourk walked down the hall to the kitchen and pulled out a soda from the fridge.

Greg had the newspaper open on the table in front of him. "Thaddeus called while you were in the shower. He wanted to let you know you were invited to Keegan's party tomorrow at three."

Rourk grinned and shook his head. Why was he not surprised? Thaddeus was something else.

Rourk woke up tense knowing that today, he would find out, for good or worse. He walked into the kitchen, where his father was sitting down with a cup of coffee.

"Dad, can I see the ring?"

"Of course, let me go grab it. It's in my room."

"Your room? I thought you always kept it in the safe."

Greg paused, then smoothly said, "Oh, well I got it out when I knew you were coming home."

Rourk poured himself a glass of orange juice while he waited, and then sat down at the table, stealing his dad's newspaper. His father came back in, holding a small green velvet box.

"Your mom would be happy to know you were passing it on."

"Hopefully passing it on. You are more positive than I am, Father."

Rourk took the box and slowly opened it. It had been years since he had looked at the ring. It was beautiful; it had been in their family for generations. He picked it up and inspected it in the light. The ruby was large and oval, set flush within the antique etchings and diamonds. It almost seemed to be glowing.

He wondered if Keegan would like it. "It is beautiful."

Greg nodded. "Yes, it is. Your mother loved that ring. I don't think she ever took it off."

Rourk glanced over and noticed his father was still wearing his simple gold wedding band. Rourk placed the ruby ring back in the box and snapped it closed. "I'm going to go for a long hike. I need to clear my mind."

Rourk looked at his watch for the hundredth time. It was now 2:30; he needed to head over to Keegan's. Taking a deep breath, he put the ring in his pocket and yelled out to his father, "I'm leaving."

"I hope it works, Rourk." His dad came to the door. "I'm proud of you, son. I know this is not easy."

Rourk grimaced and walked out the door. He climbed into his old truck and closed his eyes as he turned the key. *Please, let this work.*

He entered the long driveway at Richard's house. There were several cars parked out in front of the house. *Great.* He hadn't thought about having an audience. *Pull yourself together.*

One last deep breath and he opened the door. Stepping out of the truck, he felt his pocket to make sure the ring was still there. Head held high, he marched up to the door. He didn't even have to ring the doorbell. Thaddeus opened the door as he approached.

"So good to see you, Rourk." Thaddeus grasped his hand and smacked him on the shoulder.

"Thanks." Rourk stepped into the house and glanced around looking for Keegan, but she was not there.

"Everyone is down in the den."

Rourk's stomach was in knots as Thad led him to the den. There were a few of Keegan's friend's sitting around watching TV. The shapeshifter had his arm around Keegan and she was smiling.

Rourk wanted to rip his throat out.

"Keegan!" Thaddeus yelled.

She turned, startled, and jumped to her feet, staring wide-eyed at Rourk. "Oh."

The tiger had slithered to his feet beside her, his body tense.

Everyone's eyes were on Rourk. He was so full of conflicting emotions about seeing Keegan that he was letting their stares get to him. The faces in the room no longer looked happy. Rourk must have crashed the party.

"Hello, Keegan. I told you I would be back for you on your birthday. Here I am."

Donald stood taller and moved closer to Keegan, his arm around her shoulders. You could cut the tension in the room with a knife. The movie was playing in the background but it might as well have been complete silence.

"Rourk, I don't know what to say." Keegan shifted uncomfortably. "I thought you were still in training."

"I am. I took a weekend pass. I don't break my word." He pulled the ring out of his pocket and opened the box.

Keegan's hand flew over her mouth. She shrugged away Donald's arm and walked towards Rourk as if she was in a trance, her eyes on the ring. Once she reached him, she reached out for it, quickly pulling her hand back as if it were on fire. It was the most amazing thing she had ever seen.

"It's beautiful, just like I've always imagined it would be," she said wistfully.

Rourk's heart was in his throat. "It's yours, Keegan."

"It's so pretty. The lights are dancing all around it. Why are there sparkles coming off it?" Keegan reached up above the ring and pinched at the air, giggling.

No one in the room said a word as they watched the exchange.

"Maybe I could just try it on?"

"Of course you can." Rourk pulled it from the box, and Keegan started giggling like a little kid, bouncing on her toes.

"It's calling me. It's telling me to just put it on.

How can a ring talk?" Keegan laughed. She sounded as if she were drunk.

Rourk took her hand in his and slid the ring on her finger.

Keegan gasped, jerking her hand away from Rourk and staring wide-eyed at the ring.

"How could you? You tricked me!" Keegan yelled at Rourk, glancing back at Donald before she wrinkled her nose at the ring as if it were diseased.

Rourk stared at her confused. "Tricked you? What do you mean?"

Keegan reached up and grabbed the back of Rourk's head, pulling him to her and kissing him greedily. Almost as quickly, she shoved him away. "What did you do?"

Rourk started at her, and touched his lips.

"How could you do this to me? You didn't even give me a choice?" Keegan was freezing, goose bumps racing across her skin. She looked around the room and everyone was frozen in place except her and Rourk.

Rourk looked around the room. "Keegan, are you okay? I didn't trick you. I am your chosen. I am supposed to give you this ring on your birthday. It's tradition, you know that. I'm pretty confused myself. Why is everyone frozen?"

"A side effect of the black magic. When I get angry, I freeze things. They will be okay once I calm down." She stared down at the ring and whispered, "It's back."

"What is back?" Rourk's heart was racing.

She lifted her eyes to his. "The bond. I'm so angry at you I can't see straight. But, I want to wrap myself in you and never let you go. I've never felt so conflicted before." She glanced back at Donald, frozen in place. "I care about him."

"I can see that." Rourk glared over at Donald, his jaw clenched. He pulled her close, staring down into her blue-green eyes. "Keegan, I love you. I am your chosen. We are meant to be." He slowly traced his finger down the side of her face and outlined her full lips with his finger before he bent down to kiss her.

Keegan didn't resist. She heard the cracking, but she didn't care. She continued to kiss him as if no one else were there. She gently pulled away and whispered his name. He groaned and tangled his hands in her hair. Their eyes met for an instant, and she leaned in to kiss him again when she heard Thaddeus clear his throat.

Keegan pulled away, her cheeks flaming. Donald was standing closer than he had been, his shoulders slumped and his eyes wounded. Keegan lifted her hand towards him, then let it drop. "I'm so sorry. It's just too strong, I can't fight it."

"Can't or won't?" he said, his voice dangerously soft.

Keegan opened her mouth to reply, but noticed her brother giving Anna a high five. She jerked towards them with a glare, momentarily forgetting Donald. "You did this, didn't you?"

Anna smiled. Thaddeus just stared.

"You didn't even think of Donald's feelings." Keegan motioned to her boyfriend where he still stood, his hands limp at his sides as he glared at Thaddeus and Anna. "Or bother asking me if this is what I wanted."

"It's what was meant to be, Keegan,"

Thaddeus said, leaning against the wall.

"Who are you to say what is meant to be and what is not?"

"Keegan, chill out. We didn't do anything. The rings have always cemented the bond. All we did was make you want to try on the ring." Thaddeus glanced over at Anna. She was still smiling.

"Were you in on this?" Keegan crossed her arms and looked up at Rourk.

"No, I had no idea. However, if they had asked me I would have willingly been involved. I would have done anything to get our bond back." Rourk met her eyes.

Keegan reached for him without even thinking, her hand cupping his cheek.

Donald hung his head, taking a deep breath and letting it out. He bolted from the room, morphing into a tiger before them, knocking over furniture as he took off at full speed.

Startled, Keegan stared after him into the dim evening beyond the door. She looked back at Rourk, her heart aching.

"I'm going after Donald."

Consumed

Book 3

Keegan's Chronicles

Available Now

At all major ebook retailers, and in
print at Amazon!

Acknowledgments

A special thanks to my family for putting up with me while I write. I would also like to thank Claire Teeter and Cheryl Bradshaw for their editing skills which make this book readable. Eden Crane for the beautiful cover. Talia Jager one of my beta readers whose insight is invaluable. Last but not least I would like to thank Heather Adkins who has been a mentor to me on this writing journey. Heather beta reads, polishes, and formats she has played a huge role in making this book what it is.

About the Author

Julia Crane is the author of the <u>Keegan's Chronicles</u> series. She has a bachelor's degree in criminal justice. Julia has believed in magical creatures since the day her grandmother first told her an Irish tale. Growing up her mother greatly encouraged reading and using your imagination. Although she's spent most of her life on the US east coast, she currently lives in Dubai with her husband and three children.

Find Julia online at juliacraneauthor.com

www.ingramcontent.com/pod-product-compliance
Lightning Source LLC
Chambersburg PA
CBHW050924120626
46552CB00001B/31